A LAKE IN
DICKINSON COUNTY

W E S T L A K E O K O B O J I

By

ROSEMARY SHAW SACKETT

ISBN: 1482330938

ISBN 13:   9781482330939

Library of Congress Control Number: 2013902235
CreateSpace Independent Publishing Platform
North Charleston, South Carolina

Though altered a bit by my imagination the geographic setting is real. Lake West Okoboji is a beautiful deep blue water lake in Dickinson County in northwest Iowa just south of the Minnesota boarder. A number of people call it home while others from all parts of the United States and the world come and go. Many who grew up on the lake but now live far away return every summer seeking to experience again the magic of the summers of their youths. For many years there has been a white wooden summer cottage on Haywards Bay on the east side of the lake that was frequently available as a rental. Many years ago it was christened Tennessee for reason not known and the name has remained through many decades. The cottage is currently owned by my son Barry and his wife JoAnne.

Okoboji is a small town in Dickinson County that borders the lake, as do the towns of Arnolds Park, West Okoboji and Wahpeton. The town of Spirit Lake to the east of the lake is the county seat and Milford to the south a community where the Okoboji High School is located. In addition to West Okoboji the county plays host to a series of other small lakes and Spirit Lake the largest natural water lake in Iowa. It is West Okoboji where I found the magic that I dare to say many have shared. My husband and I were introduced to it in early childhood and not long after our marriage we built a house next to Tennessee and made it our home. My five children grew up on the lake and it is their love. My daughter was married on its shore and my oldest son on its water. Murphy my oldest son is a character in the book and as did the character he once had a Bar in Arnolds Part called Murphys and he was recognized for his skills in water sports.

The poems attributed to Adelia and others are my poems.

PREFACE

Two million years ago glaciers began covering what is now Iowa with their icy grips. On the path of the last glacier, the Des Moines Lobe that expanded into Iowa from the vast Wisconsinan ice sheet, the lakes of Iowa occurred. One lake deeper and more beautiful than the rest was the chosen home of the water spirits. The lake an attraction to the Paleo-Indians, the first persons to come to the area as the glacier melted, and the Indian tribes that followed through the centuries came to be called Okoboozhy.

June 1858

The vast western sky was painted barely pink by a sun that minutes before slipped below the horizon dwarfing the man standing on a high bank committing to memory the beauty of Okoboozhy that had bathed, soothed and delighted him. Before the sun rose he would leave this land of sweeping prairies, tall grasses, plentiful game and fish to follow his father and brothers to places unknown.

The dimming light reflected on his red skin and somber pocked face. He should stay and protect the land of his ancestors from the rages of men of white face who came in large number. His body weakened by the cursed illness that pitted his face he could not fight. The white man had taken his land. They were taking this beautiful water. A memory of the lake would forever be with him. He must punish those driving him away.

He raised his hands and shouted to the spirits beneath the calm water until he awoke a storm and the waves broke madly and grew wild, dark and angry.

He left not seeing the maiden watching him from the covering on the shore. She there with the boy of white skin who for many moon she met on the bank where they frolicked in the water and ran in the sand. She too would soon leave and never return to these waters where she and the boy learned of love. Their tongues strange his body warmed hers in the storming night. She shared the Brave's anger at being driven away but he had been selfish in leaving a curse. The waters before her belonged to no one. The beauty of the lake great it must remain a place of love and magic for all who saw the lake's wonder. The brave's curse had to be broken.

She must act before the sun rose high in the sky. In early morning she gathered petals of sweet wild flowers, the shell of a robin's egg and the leaf of an oak tree. She stood on the bank where the Brave had stood and whispered in soft voice to the water spirits. As she threw the petals, egg shell and leaf to the water the waves subsided. The lake laid a silent mirror reflecting the light spreading the eastern sky.

She speaking in her tongue told the boy of white skin of the Brave's curse and that she had spoken with the water spirits and broken it. She told him the lake carried a promise of return for those who found love by these waters. She knew he understood.

The maiden mounted her small horse and rode to join her family traveling west. Grieving that the color of their skin would forever keep she and the boy apart in life in her heart she carried the promise of the water spirits that in death on this lake their souls would reunite.

My name is Karen Good and I came to write this story about a woman I never met, the first man with whom I fell in love, a lake called Okoboji and a summer cottage someone named Tennessee after I started working as a legal secretary for Charlie Hogan in his law office two doors from the post office in Okoboji, a small Iowa town that bustles in summer due to its location on the eastern shore of Lake West Okoboji.

My introduction to this lake that appears as an oasis in flat corn and bean fields of northwest Iowa came in June of my thirteenth summer. My father an attorney with Standard Insurance headquartered in Des

Moines, Iowa, decided his family needed a summer at Okoboji. As my father did he first rented a rambling old frame summer cottage someone had christened 'Tennessee' on Haywards Bay on the east side of the lake. Only after the lease was signed did he tell my mother, my older brother and I, we would spend the summer there.

Angered my father had spoiled my summer I spent the first week at Okoboji sitting under a tall burr oak tree sulking. By the second week my father had enrolled me in sailing lessons at the Okoboji Yacht Club on Dixon Beach. Meeting Chip the six foot two blond haired sailing instructor with slate blue eyes immediately improved my summer. I so taken with him I actually listened as he lectured to us about the lake, the winds, and sailboats. It was there I met Ellie, Elizabeth and Kittie. We all were in love with Chip. It was my best growing up summer.

On hot windless days Chip set a blackboard up out side and detailed the characteristics of the classes of boats that sailed in competition on West Okoboji. I was most interested in the X Boat, sixteen foot long and raced by those less than sixteen years of age. Ellie's family owned controlling interest in Standard Insurance. Elizabeth and Kittie and I took turns crewing for her on her X boat and listening to her talk of her family's money.

Chip also told us about other boats, the C's and the M16's and the M20's and the E's sailed by the older sailors. More interested in Chip than the boats my dreams were full of him.

The spring I turned fourteen my brother graduated from Roosevelt High School and would attend Buena Vista College in the fall. Beg as I did my father said we could not afford to rent Tennessee that summer with college expenses staring him in the face.

Four years later I was to enroll at the University of Iowa in Iowa City some three hundred miles from Okoboji. Yet during my college years at the University my friends and I would, in the summer, drive the three hundred miles from Iowa City to Okoboji for a weekend. I could never wait to go and never wanted to leave looking and occasionally finding for a brief moment the magic of my thirteenth summer.

Just before my senior year several sorority sisters and I went to Okoboji on a July weekend when the thermometer never dropped below ninety degrees. We camped in a tent pitched at Green Acres, a state campground on the west side of the lake. Saturday night we dressed in the public bathroom. Wearing sleeveless starched cotton dresses with gathered shirts and can cans stiffened with sugar starch, we ratted our hair, blued our eye lids and sprayed ourselves with green perfume. We had reserved a booth at the Roof Garden, a second floor ballroom, over arcades, a fun house, shops and the Merry-go-Round bar at Arnolds Park Amusement Park on the southeast shore of West Okoboji. A rock and roll band whose name I no longer remember played the twist most of the night. Not one of the awkward young men circling the floor and eye balling the girls asked me to dance. Feeling rejected I went down to the state pier to cool off after having my hand stamped to assure reentry.

Sitting there wishing I dare take off my garter belt and nylons and dangle my bare feet in the water I looked up to see a tall curly head man walk on the pier. He said good evening and purposely looked away. I got brave and asked him where he was from and he told me he grew up in Clinton on the other side of the state by the Mississippi River and went to Iowa State University in Ames. His name was Roger.

I talked about returning to the dance. Roger suggested we take a walk. We stopped by the fun house watching a funny wooden clown pretending to play a piano. We spent twenty cents for tickets for a ride on a little train and rode it two circles around the park. Finally we went to the Peacock Lounge and drank Miller's beer from frosty bottles and put the golden bands from the top of the bottles around our fingers. That was the last time I saw Chip.

I was on the way back from the bathroom and saw him standing at the bar seemingly alone. I said hello. He said hello and then hesitated like he should know me but wasn't sure. I explained I had been in his sailing class nearly a decade earlier. His slate blue eyes twinkled and he said, "You turned into a beautiful woman."

I beamed and was ready to continue my conversation as Roger joined us. Roger was staying with neighbors of Chip so they knew each other and talked. On the way out I mentioned to Roger Chip looked unhappy. Roger said Chip told him the night before about I girl he fell in love with when he was a sailing instructor and his quest to find her. I blushed hoping Roger did not see.

By Halloween Roger and I were pinned and at New Years engaged. We married at St. John's Basilica on University Avenue in Des Moines on a hot August tenth. Roger sent an invitation to Chip but he did not come. Nor did we see him when we honeymooned at the New Inn a resort on West Okoboji and made love for the first time. There three days thanks to a generous check from my grandmother we rode the excursion boat, the Queen, skated to organ music at the Majestic Skating Rink and after midnight swam nude in the tepid lake water.

Two weeks later we started our teaching careers at DMT Consolidated School, a township school in Pocahontas County in northwest Iowa. I taught English and Roger history. I coached declam and directed the junior and senior class plays and was yearbook sponsor. Roger coached boys' basketball and track. Thirty-three years later our children Jeff, Heather and Randy were out of college and I was still teaching English. Roger gave up the classroom years earlier and was the superintendent of a middle-sized school district. The school district merged with another and he lost his job.

We tightened our belts and took early retirement deciding to move to Okoboji. Neither of us mentioned it then but we each carried the hope we could recapture the magic of our youth. Lots and homes on West Lake Okoboji too expensive we chose a condominium decorated in every shade of beige from eggshell to sand on East Okoboji, a smaller adjoining lake, and settled in.

Roger took a part time job at the area community college. I answered Charlie Hogan's ad for a legal secretary. Charlie seeing I had been an English teacher hired me on the spot.

Charlie born in Chicago and his wife Jane a native of the area were both educated at the University of Virginia. Charlie said the first time he came to Okoboji he felt a pull to stay. He said it felt more like home than any place he had ever lived, it was where he should always be. He said he was not sure why. It was just a strange thing.

Jane originally obtained a teaching job but now stayed home with their young daughter named Adelia Elizabeth after both her grandmothers. As Charlie told me that he got teary eyed but said nothing more.

One day in a cozy little coffee shop called BROADWAY BREW on Broadway Street a several block long street in Arnolds Park I looked for a long time at a woman about my age sipping a large cup of the house brew. Katie the owner called her Ellie. I recognized my childhood friend. We hugged and rejoiced in our reunion. I related I was working for Charlie. Ellie cried a bit and told me his mother Adelia had become a great friend and she still mourned her death.

I must have looked puzzled as Ellie went on to tell me Adelia and her second husband were killed in an airplane crash returning from a week honeymoon cruise in Alaska several years earlier.

"Adelia never got to meet her granddaughter, Ellie stated. It has been hard on Charlie and Jane losing both of their mothers so close together. Jane talked to me one day about how she so wished her daughter had a grandmother. Adelia would have adored the little girl, she concluded."

"Both mothers?"

Ellie noted my confusion. "Elizabeth was Jane's mother. Poor dear died of lung cancer. Smoked herself to death. She started when you stole your father's Lucky Strikes and we almost burned down my grandmother's boathouse. She never stopped. I hope you did."

"I did," I responded not certain what to say.

"I loved Elizabeth like a sister. Her husband is a dear friend."

I wanted to ask how dear but Ellie changed the subject.

Charlie came to rely on me. I felt closer to him after my conversation with Ellie. He was a fine man and I found satisfaction assisting him and developed a close relationship with a number of his clients. Many were older and needed a kind hand to help them untangle business matters. I worked with students all my adult life. Few were as grateful for assistance as Charlie's clients. Some needed so much. One of those was Agnes Luc.

Charlie sent me to Lakeview nursing home on occasion to see Agnes Charlie's stepfather's mother. He felt an obligation to help her. She told me often she had no living relatives and it was hard to think about dying when you left no one behind.

One afternoon Charlie had taken off to sail and a man called telling me a piece of luggage found after the plane crash was identified as belonging to Charlie's mother. He wished to deliver it if Charlie would set a time.

I told Charlie about the call; he said anguish in his voice. "Tell him I don't want it."

I relayed Charlie's message to the man. He told me to tell Charlie there were personal papers in the luggage, an old blue train case. He made it clear Charlie would want the papers.

I hated to tell Charlie what the man said remembering the anguish he experienced the first time we talked about his mother's luggage but I did. In a voice void of emotion he said, "Oh her train case. Tell him to send it. One day I will be strong enough to look in it."

The train case was delivered to Charlie's office. A small rectangular piece of blue luggage it opened at the top, had a mirror on it lid and could be carried like a purse. It probably got it name because its size allowed women traveling by train to put their make up in it and keep it at their seats for easy access. After it was delivered it sat for several weeks on a back file at the office. I was curious but said nothing. One afternoon just after closing time Charlie approached me. "Would you take the train case?" he asked.

"Oh course." I hesitated and he continued.

"Mother kept that train case close for as long as I can remember. She said her grandmother bought it for her with Green stamps something some stores gave when you spent money there. I believe mother kept her writings and letters in it. I was in high school when I tried to open the case. She caught me before I had seen anything. In one of her only angry moments she forbad me to look in it again. Then the day before she married my stepfather she told me when she died I was to look at the papers in the train case. She said it would be important to me. She hesitated then before telling me I was not to think less of anyone after I had. It was a strange instruction. I didn't think about it again until you told me the case had been found."

Charlie stopped talking. I stood waiting. Finally he continued, "I can't look in there. I'm not strong enough. Maybe you would and summarize for me what you find. It would be less traumatic to read on a typed page than in my mother's hand. She wrote poems. I laughed at her about them. Some of them were good. I never told her that and it is a guilt I carry."

"Of course I will Charlie," I too quickly replied. The mystery of the train case intrigued me. I took the blue train case home. It was identical to the green one my grandmother gave me for high school graduation that I discarded years ago. The outside of this case showed signs of scorching heat. The mirror inside was broken and fragments of glass had found their way in the satin lining. Wearing gloves I went thought the papers one by one. Some were difficult to read. Others were clear.

I found diary entries, scrapes of dated paper, letters and poems, the remaining record of the life of a private woman. Reading I felt Adelia's emotions. At times I felt her scolding me for delving into her private places. I cried a lot thinking she was dead and knew we would be friends if she were alive.

A four-line diary entry drove me to learn more about the early history of the lake. On a cool summer afternoon I wandered to the Gardner log cabin near the amusement park. There in March of 1857 thirty-three white men, women and children were murdered by the Native American Inkpaduta and his followers in the bloodiest battle in recorded Iowa history. The curator at the site was studying the history of the Indian movement and the often-unfair treatment the Native Americans received from the white man. A young woman of Native American descent examining the exhibits told me she had driven from Oklahoma to Okoboji. She said some unknown force had brought her to West Lake Okoboji. Then she related a tale passed down in her family from mother to daughter telling that the soul of her great-great- great-great-great grandmother returned to this lake where it joined the soul of an early white settler's son who she fell in love with and left in her youth when her family was forced west and she never forgot him. I found her stories so interesting I wanted to write them and nearly forgot my promise to Charlie.

Ellie kept me on track. I met her many days before I went to work generally over a cup of coffee at Broadway Brew. I questioned her about the Adelia she knew. The reward of rekindling a friendship with an old friend was Adelia's gift to me. I pondered over my gift to her and how to share with her son the life I was learning she led.

After reading every diary entry, letter, scrap of paper and poem I knew I had to write Adelia's story. Some days when I wrote, I laughed. On others I cried. Sifting through the contents of the train case I had stood witness to a life of love and acceptance. I learned the strange secret that brought Charlie to Okoboji. Most importantly I learned one has to treasure the precious gift of love.

Finally I took the story peppered with her poems to Charlie. "I wrote your mother's story," I said simply.

Anger flashed in Charlie's slate blue eyes, "I wanted a summary not a story."

"Charlie," I shouted, "your mothers life deserves a story. I stopped. We looked at each other both embarrassed by the emotions we had unleashed.

There was a long silence before Charlie said softly, "I loved her but she had no story. It can't be interesting. She was a perfect woman. Always did what was right. She was so much better than I could ever be. She died free of sin. She was so pure sometime I thought... I interrupted him. "Charlie children don't know their parents' secrets."

"I knew my mother." Charlie was defensive. I had invaded his privacy. I said nothing more but he continued, " We were close. I was her only child. My father was too old for her and she confided in me always."

He took the manuscript and walked off. That closed our conversation. I started worrying about what I had written.

ADELIA'S STORY

CHAPTER I

The youth, the love, the place
a recollection, or a dream
Was it so sweet or have
the many days since then
erased the flaws leaving
etched the perfect memory?

ADELIA HOGAN

ARNOLDS PARK IOWA JUNE 1963

Standing bare footed on the rough oak board floor in the Arnolds Park Grocery, the fresh scrubbed girl looked younger than her seventeen years. Softly her left hand brushed sun streaked blond hair from her eyes as she picked plump dark red Bing cherries from a wooden crate on the counter. Showing each cherry to a tanned bobbed hair child in an expensive play suit only if the child nodded approval did the girl put the fruit in a brown paper bag. Near a display of tinned tomatoes a boy not yet nineteen stood. He was tall, well over six feet. Blond hair curled on his forehead, his slate blue eyes were riveted on the girl picking out the fruit.

The bag half full she handed it to a hefty woman in a dirty butcher apron who stood with her back to shelves of canned goods and twenty-five pound sacks of flour. The woman put the bag on the scale. The girl dug deep in the pocket of her tight cut off blue jeans before bringing forth three quarters, one dime and two cents to pay.

Outside on Broadway Street June sun beat on the sidewalk. The child patted a big yellow Labrador lounging near the building before the girl put the child in a red wagon and headed toward the sparkling lake. They crossed railroad tracks the child laughing at the bumps and quickly passed the Peacock Lounge where the smell of last night's stale beer reached the sidewalk. Approaching the Kiddie amusement park the child begged to ride a carved wooden horse on the big carousel. A lone boy rode in one of connecting miniature boats floating in a circle of stagnant water. On the lake, The Queen, once a proud steam ship and now a tired excursion boat diesel powered competing with the Empress a shinny new barge for business, had left its dock. The five passengers on board all stood on the top deck.

At the Amusement Park near the Fun House the child jumped from the wagon. After the child took a life jacket from the wagon and the girl put it on the child did the two run to the end of the state pier. There they sat feet dangling in the water as each took a cherry from the paper sack and twisting off the stem slowly ate the tasty fruit before spitting the pit far into the lake. "To grow cherry trees," the child said.

They ate all but five of the cherries before the girl looked up and saw the boy from the grocery store the big yellow dog at his side. He appeared to be shy and said nothing. The dog went to the child. The boy's eyes met the girl's. She bade him sit and handed him a cherry. He slowly ate the fruit before spitting the pit in the lake. The small child giggled and hugged the dog. The boy's face reddened. The girl smiled. No words were exchanged. Bug remembered it as the day she fell in love.

Back at the Hamilton's three story white frame cottage on West Okoboji where Bug worked as a summer girl, the boy never left her thoughts. Hamilton's owned the cottage, five Hardware stores in South Dakota and a home on the Prairie Gold Club in Lincoln, Nebraska. They hired a summer girl to watch Sara and Billie and help Karla Hamilton with household chores.

The Hamiltons flew an Okoboji Yacht Club flag next to a University of Nebraska flag at the end of their dock. Billie Hamilton took sailing lessons with Jeffery Kettleson, his next-door neighbor. Billie raced his X class sailboat in the Yacht Club races Wednesday afternoon, Saturday afternoon and Sunday morning. Jeffery Kettleson served as his crew. Jeffery's father, Dr. Kettleson, as he insisted he be called, was an orthodontist in Sioux City. He left his wife Betty with Jeffery at the lake the entire summer joining them only on occasional weekends.

The Kettleson had not had a summer girl for three years. There was whispering it was because the Dr. crawled in bed with the last summer girl and it took a big sum to convince her family not to have criminal charges filed against the doctor.

Mrs. Kettleson and Karla were friends and on Thursday morning the two ladies left Bug with the three children and went to the Red Owl grocery Store in Spirit Lake the county seat. They returned about a quarter past ten the car full of paper sacks with the Red Owl trademark filled with a week's supply of groceries. Bug help Karla put away her purchases before she helped Mrs. Kettleson. Then she and Mrs. Kettleson would fix lunch and the evening meal for the group. Bug quickly grew fond of Mrs. Kettleson who treated Bug with respect and shared cooking tips and her favorite receipts.

Friday mornings Bug stripped the sheets off the beds in the Hamilton cottage. The sheets made two loads for the Bendix automatic washer on the back-screened porch. Sunny days Karla demanded Bug hang the sheets out on the long cloths line in back. She did allow the cases to go in the Maytag dryer. Karla fretted that her washer and dryer were not a matched pair.

Bug nearly always cooked the evening meal. She called it dinner. Karla called it supper and said the noon meal was dinner. Bug served the family in the big dinning room overlooking the lake. She ate alone at a small table in the kitchen.

Monday afternoon at four Bug was off until Tuesday afternoon at four. The first three weeks knowing no one but the Hamiltons she hung around their cottage. The Hamilton's treated her stiffly so she spent her free time in her room over the garage writing poems in her lined composition book. She wrote of the lake, and the sunsets and the oak leaves. She penned letters on pink scented stationary to her grandmother and Mary Claire O'Brien, her best friend since fourth grade at Blessed Sacrament School. In fifth grade Bug and Mary Claire decided to be nuns after Sister Mary Catherine, who had friendly brown eyes and a loving smile, talked to them about religious vocations. By the time they went to St. Monica's Academy as high school freshman most of their Blessed Sacrament classmates had boy friends and talked about going steady and the man they would marry. Yet Mary Claire and Bug held fast to their conviction to join a holy order.

Bug attended St. Monica's six weeks before Michael McMahon from Catholic Boys' High asked her to the Homecoming dance. Bug told Michael she was going to be a nun and didn't go out with boys. Michael called her nun after that and no other asked her to a dance.

At St. Monica's in the girls' bathroom next to the music room Bug listened to the girls with boyfriends talk about parking and French kissing. A senior hinted of going all the way. Bug thought she knew what that meant but was not sure. She asked Mary Claire if she wanted to be with a boy. Mary Claire said it would be disgusting and she would never do the things a boy made you do. Bug said out loud yes she agreed but wasn't certain she meant it. Some days she regretted not going to the dance with Michael McMahon, but she never told Mary Claire.

In the fall Mary Claire would enter St. Bernadette's Convent. Bug wanted to go but there was no money for the tuition the school charged. Bug would finish her senior year at St. Monica's where members of the parish paid nothing to attend.

Bug feeling badly that she couldn't join Mary Claire listened to her grandmother's friend whose daughter and husband summered at Lake Okoboji in Iowa. She suggested Bug apply for the job of a summer girl with Hamiltons because it paid well and would be good for Bug to get out of the city for the summer. Bug wrote a letter of application. Karla interviewed her on the telephone before she offered the job. There was a weekly paycheck and a round trip bus ticket from Chicago to Arnold's Park Iowa.

Bug's grandmother had tears in her eyes at the bus station and hugged Bug very tight telling her how much she loved her and warned her to be careful of young men who sought her favors.

The day Bug gave the boy with the yellow dog a cherry on the pier she forgot about wanting to go to the convent. He rarely left her thoughts.

Monday of the third week Billie announced he would not go to sailing school unless Bug went with him. Karla told her to go. Bug had to follow Karla's instructions.

Bug sat on the sand beach near the Okoboji Yacht Club building on Dixon Beach near a sprawling resort called the New Inn. A healthy wind blew across the lake. Billie and six other boys and seven girls sailed Lasars, one-person single sailboats, off the shore. The boy, who shared her cherries their sailing instructor, wore a tight swimming suit that showed his tanned muscular legs and other things. He drove a Boston Whaler boat and yelled instructions through a megaphone at the young sailors over the wind. Billie told Bug his name was Chip. She never took her eyes off him.

Billie begged for Bug to go to his next sailing lesson. Billie generally didn't want Bug near him but he wanted her at his sailing lessons. She said she would like to go. She wanted Karla to let her. But Karla said no explaining Bug had to wash the windows on the big porch overlooking the lake.

The next Monday Karla was gone when Billie was scheduled for sailing school. Billie told Bug, his sailing instructor promised to take him out in his class C sail boat if he brought Bug to sailing school. Bug smiled and took Sara and went with Billie.

The day was still. The lake mirror smooth and the sails on the Lasars hung limp. Chip wore smart white shorts. He gave a chalk talk using the big black board in the Yacht Club building. Bug stayed out on the beach with Sara and the Chip's dog Rex.

The sailing school students grew restless. Chip brought them outside. He sat by Bug and smiled. Her face reddened. She smiled back. "I am glad you came," he said looking straight in her eyes. She looked down and said nothing. She did not tell him about the times since the day on the pier she had thought about him. There was an uncomfortable silence before he spoke again, " There is a dance at the Roof Garden tomorrow night go with me."

Flustered she said nothing. He said it a second time and told her a band called The Critckets from Lubbock Texas were playing. She didn't tell him like she told Michael McMahon that she was going to be a nun. Instead she said, "I'll ask Karla."

"Say you will go. I will ask Karla," he persisted.

"I would like to," she said shyly hoping he did not hear her heart thumping in her chest. He didn't hear her all the way back to the Hamilton's softly saying Chip, Chip, Chip over and over.

Chip had said he would pick Bug up at eight. Bug said nothing to Karla yet she asked Bug what she was wearing to the dance and Bug knew Chip kept his promise. Bug said she did not know what to wear.

Karla offered her a pale blue sundress and a strapless bra with padded cups and stays Chip must have liked the sundress. Bug came in the living room where he waited. He looked her over carefully before saying, "You are gorgeous."

The band played. The Roof Garden was crowded. Bug had never danced with a boy before. Sometimes the girls at her school would dance with each other while the nuns explained one should never dance close to a boy. But Chip and Bug danced close. Being in Chip's arms felt good. Chip brought Bug home before midnight and gently kissed her lips before she went in the door.

After that night Chip and Rex spent hours at Karla and Lou's. Bug thought Karla and Lou would mind. They didn't. They liked Chip and started treating Bug better. If Chip stayed for dinner Karla told Bug to set a place for herself in the dinning room. Billie adored Chip. Some times Bug thought Karla did too. On the sunny days Chip didn't teach sailing he arrived at the Hamilton's dock in his parents mahogany planked Chris-Craft inboard with red leather seats. Other times he drove his yellow Mercury convertible, Rex always on the seat beside him. Sunday afternoons Chip took Bug and the children to the Arnolds Park Amusement Park. They ate nutty bars; a square of hard vanilla ice cream covered with sweet chocolate and chopped peanuts and ate black walnut taffy after watching a machine in the window of the candy shop pull the confection into thin white ropes. The children played skee ball near the nutty bar stand while Chip and Bug sat on a bench near the roller coaster Rex at their feet. Chip held Bug close and gently kissed her lips when they thought no one was looking. Rex jealous would nestle between them. Bug treasured Chip's kisses. She woke at night thinking how they felt. At her desk she wrote his name with Mrs. in front practicing for it to be her name.

Mid July Mary Claire sent application papers for a new scholarship that would pay all the costs at St. Bernadette's Convent school and wrote that Bug had a good chance of getting the scholarship and they could be in Convent school together. Bug didn't tell Mary Claire about Chip. She answered she should stay at St. Monica's another year to be close to her grandmother.

There were other dances at the Roof Garden. The special one was in late August when a group of five young men from Hawthorne, California, who called themselves 'The Beach Boys', played the venue. It was their first tour one of the boys' father having brought the group cross country in a station wagon pulling a trailer. It was a special night both Chip and Bug loved the Beach Boys sound and Bug was sure she had never seen a better-looking group of band members.

Soon it was the last week of August. Bug's return ticket was for the next Monday on the bus leaving from the Arnolds Park school corner at three o'clock in the afternoon. Sunday Dr. Kettleson would take Billie and Jeffery to Camp Foster on Lake East Okoboji. Bug washed and ironed and packed Billie's cloths. Sunday for breakfast she fixed Billie's favorite breakfast French toast and sausage patties served with cold melon.

Billie and Jeffery wanted Bug to see their camp. Dr. Kettleson said she should come. She helped Billie carry his suitcase to a small cabin in the woods and waited as he unpacked. She wondered why Karla had her iron his cloths. They wouldn't stay pressed very long.

Dr. Kettleson drove a strange route back stopping on a vacant drive way and putting his hand on Bug's leg. Bug asked Dr. Kettleson why they stopped. He said he thought she wanted to stop. She said she didn't that Chip was waiting for her at Hamilton's. Dr. Kettleson looked mad yet stayed parked. "You sure are pretty," he said grabbing her and bringing her close to his body. She struggled as he kissed her putting his hands on her breasts and finally pulling off her shorts and white cotton panties fondling her private parts before opening the fly on his pants and sticking his penis inside her. Bug willed herself elsewhere. She lost track of time but finally he zipped up his fly started the car and drove off while Bug tears filling her eyes sought to pull on her panties and shorts. They drove to the Hamilton's cottage in silence and Dr. Kettleson pulled in his driveway and turned off his car and exited it leaving Bug alone with her tears. Finally she took a deep breath got out of the car and quietly went in the backdoor of the Hamilton cottage hoping to find Chip but knowing she was too embarrassed to confide in him if her were there. He could not know what Dr. Kettleson had done to her.

Once inside Karla told her Chip had come with Réx but couldn't wait. Noting Bug's tearstained face Karla told Bug it was nothing to cry about and that she needed to think about getting back to Chicago.

Taking Karla's heed Bug went to her room and began packing her clothing in cardboard boxes. She wished for luggage. Many times she told her grandmother she had to have the blue Samsonite luggage advertised in *Seventeen* magazine. It seemed everybody in her school had the luggage but she did not.

As Bug finished packing she heard Chip downstairs talking to Karla. He called to Bug telling her they were going swimming. She pulled on her black one-piece swimming suit covering it with a white shirt. Chip drove his family's Chris Craft inboard away from the dock finally putting down the anchor. Bug, Chip and Rex jumped in the warm lake water. Finally tired Rex lay on the deck. Bug and Chip went in the cabin of the boat. She snuggled with Chip and for the first time he put his hand under her swimming suit and touched her breast. Slowly Chip took off her swimming suit. She did not as she did so many other times try to stop him. Finally she lay naked before him. He kissed her body. She was sinning but her body ached for him as she watched him pull off his swimming trunks. She knew she should make him stop but could not. She let him inside her hoping it would ease the pain of Dr. Kettleson's actions but it did not. When they put their swimming suits back on and went to the deck of the boat Rex looked at her strangely. She felt over whelming guilt. Today in the course of a few hours she had committed two mortal sins and her soul was stained. All the way to shore she silently said the Act of Contrition.

Chip was silent until Bug got off the boat then he said he would take her to the bus. He didn't take her hand, hold her close or kiss her as he always had. She sensed it was because she had been easy. She feared he did not respect her any more. She had lost herself respect.

Mid-evening Karla took Bug and Sara to the Ice Cream Shop on Broadway Street. Karla promised Bug a banana split on her last day of work. Bug ordered her banana split with chocolate, strawberry and pineapple topping and lots of nuts and whipped crème and cherries. She ate one bite before she saw Chip's yellow convertible. He was driving and a girl with long dark hair in the front seat sat nearly on his lap. Rex was not in the car. Bug couldn't swallow the ice cream. The banana split in her hands made her sick. Back at Hamilton's she flushed it down the toilet. Banana splits were expensive. She did not want Karla to think her ungrateful.

Chip called Bug early Monday morning. Bug told him Karla was taking her to the bus. She never knew why she did not listen for his response. She never got over wishing she had.

CHAPTER II

JUNE 2, 1993

Mother,

Jane has her mother, father, brothers, sisters, cousins, aunts, and uncles. You are all the family I have. You are coming. No excuses. I have engaged a cottage for you on the lakeshore for twelve weeks. The cottage is named Tennessee. The oak trees are beautiful. I need you, mom. I really need you. Charlie

Fingering the silver bracelet on her left wrist Adelia Hogan looked out the window at the patchwork of black dirt and green fields. United flight 612 from Chicago was beginning its descent to Des Moines International Airport. Her train case securely at her feet the vacant seat beside her was a painful reminder Joe, her husband of twenty-eight years, was dead. The ache of her loneliness intensified as she felt the wheels of the plane touch the ground.

Adelia first saw the green Iowa plains through the window of a dusty tired bus when she still bubbled with youthful enthusiasm. But for the letter from her only child she would never have returned.

The medium sized terminal had clean floors and white faces. People looked in each other's eyes. Smiles and greetings were frequent. Strangers to Adelia the people had an easy way of smiling, saying hello. She sensed she had come on a family reunion. Charlie warned her not to talk about people in Iowa. "It seems all Iowans are related to each other, they are all one family," he cautioned. She would never be a member of this family. At the United Express counter she confirmed her connecting flight to Spencer, Iowa, some twenty miles south of Okoboji and found herself shaking her mind full of anticipation mixed with fear. Clutching her train case she sat alone near a window staring at a yellow bus with bold black letter saying "Des Moines Catholic Schools." Children wearing uniform blue pants and white shirts were unloading. A man's voice behind her asking if she were going to Spencer interrupted her thoughts. She nodded without turning.

"Have you business there?" He persisted. "No," she spoke firmly intending the tone of her voice to signal she did not want to be bothered.

Adelia stood and walked to the window. If Joe were here, she would not feel alone. Stooped, gray, at the lake home they had on lake Tahoe Joe wore plaid flannel shirts and left the shirttails hanging out. When he looked at her, she saw the love and pride in his eyes. Always he guarded her from other men. He told them she was his wife. She longed to hear those words from his lips today though she no longer remembered the sound of his voice. The day they married in the wedding chapel near Lake Tahoe Joe paid extra for recorded organ music and fresh cut flowers. The minister who married them had a lisp and got the hiccups. Adelia once dreamed of a white wedding dress, a big cathedral and six attendants in flowing pink gowns. At Tahoe the attendant beside her came for an extra charge and wore an aqua dress with a broken zipper. After the minister pronounced them husband and wife Joe kissed her while she dreamed of a different groom. Over the years there would be the continued dream of a different ceremony. One planned with friends and mounds of sweet daisies, buttercups, small roses, and a Champaign toast. One with a different groom.

Joe was dead. She was a widow before she was fifty having married a man twenty-five years her senior. She felt guilty entertaining these thoughts. No man could have been better to her than Joe.

"You look familiar." A man came and stood beside her. Did she look familiar? A panic came. A voice announced a plane to Chicago was loading. She reached for her train case. She would be on that plane. The man kept talking, "What are you doing in Spencer?" His body was between hers and the ticket counter. She pretended she did not hear. "Seeing relatives?" he persisted.

How could anyone be this intrusive? Charlie said Iowans were that way. They asked personal questions. They thought they knew you when they didn't. She took a deep breath before the panic subsided.

"Sorry I didn't mean to pry." The man's voice apologetic she felt guilty not responding. She swallowed, turned, almost smiled and said, "a wedding," before her eyes returned to looking at the school bus unloading children. One small blond boy stood crying. She remembered how often Charlie cried. He quit quickly if Joe held him. He loved Joe.

"Oh, who's wedding?"

His interest was spurred. In Chicago no one asked such questions. In Chicago no one cared who you were or what you did. There were too many faces there to care about one. No one there ever really looked you in the eye.

She hesitated and with difficulty finally said "Jane Abbott's."

He responded quickly "Misses and I attended the engagement party Elizabeth and Andrew had for the couple last winter. Jane is a great girl. Old Andrew and Elizabeth did themselves proud with their kids.

"This stranger had been at her son's engagement party. She claimed illness and did not come. In was only the second time he had not attended one of Charlie's events, the debate and track meets, the baseball, football, band concerts, and plays. Whether Charlie was the star sitting on the bench or hidden in the back row, she had been there. This stranger was at a party for Charlie and she was not. Her sins kept her away. This man liked Jane. She tried to shut him out but the man continued his inquisition, "How do you know them?" If only he would leave her alone. It was not his business.

She hesitated before she said, "Charlie is my son."

"You have a good boy. You did a good job raising him."

"Thank you do you know Jane well?" She surprised herself talking to him, saying Jane's name. The man had complimented her. Since Joe died no one complimented her. She had millions of dollars but no compliments. Money did not buy compliments. Joe had been so generous with them. That was what she missed most.

"Name is John Holland, I grew up at Okoboji with Jane's mother. We raced sailboats. Her sailboat was P5. Mine was P6. Elizabeth was my first love."

The panic came. Adelia stood close to the window until a tall woman her ample hips pushing the seams of her navy blue uniform called the flight to Spencer. She bit her lip and followed John Holland outside to the small plane waiting in the landing area. She boarded first. An attendant told her she needed to check her train case. She watched him carefully as he tagged it and put it in the front hold.

Adelia sat in the first seat in the fifteen-passenger plane. John Holland winked as he came down the isle. She smiled and was relieve he was in the back. She opened her billfold and pulled out a ragged picture of two smiling teens. She started at the faces a long time before turning the picture over where she reread for the thousandth time the words 'Love you Bug' printed in bold letters followed by 'Chip' in a scrawled signature. How she got the nickname Bug she couldn't remember but after she married Joe she never used it again.

The landscape darkened in the sixty-minute flight to Spencer. By the time they landed the sun was but a pink streak in the western sky. Adelia was relieved to exit the plane and have some one handed her the train case. She clutched it tightly.

CHAPTER   III

April 2, 1964

Dear Diary,

Joe took me to the Holy Family Hospital at six this morning. It was long and hard but finally he came at four minutes after nine. He measured nineteen and one half inches long and weighed seven pounds seven and one half ounces. Joe met me when I came out of the delivery room. He knew it was a boy and asked he be named after Charlie O'Malloy. We met at Charlie's Diner. Charlie died two months ago in the emergency room of Holy Family. I wanted to name him Troy but agreed to Charlie. Joe called his office and said I had a boy and the only thing that had ever made him happier was marrying me. Joe stayed with me a while until the snippy nurse on the three to eleven shift told him to go because I needed rest. I want to see my baby again. I have yet to hold him. I didn't believe I could love another human being this much. I must always protect my child. **ADELIA HOGAN**

Adelia's eyes scanned the waiting area for a familiar face praying the one she saw would be Charlie's. Hopeful if it were not that her darkened hair, pierced ears, and expensive cloths would be taken for those of a stranger. John Holland embraced a slim woman wearing a cotton dress with pink and red flowers on a purple background. He said something to her before they looked toward Adelia. They were talking about her. The panic started then she saw Charlie hurrying in the door. He seemed to be alone. She took a deep breath and rushed to his side.

15

In the twenty minute drive in the dark to the town of Okoboji where Charlie had reserved a room for her at the New Inn on West Okoboji Lake until the cottage he had engaged was vacant, he thanked her many times for coming. Then he outlined the events of the next weeks. Tired she barely listened, haunting words ringing in her head.

Charlie checked Adelia in the resort and carried her bags to a room on the lakeshore. He chided her about always bringing her train case and told her she looked tired before promising to pick her up at ten the next morning to take her to a small restaurant for homemade buttermilk pancakes.

Alone she carefully put the train case in the corner. She unpacked her over night bag and washed her face before going to the porch outside. The night still she savored the sweet smell of lake air. The skies black she stared at a field of scattered stars. Memories she thought she had erased of other nights looking at stars in a big sky flooded back and relit a spark that once burned inside her.

Frightened by her feeling she hurried inside and closed the curtain to hide the lake from her view. After quickly writing in her diary she undressed, soaked in a hot tub and putting on an ivory lace nightgown pulled the spread down and lay on the sheets listening to the occasional motorboat and happy young voices from the lake. Her eyes moist she longed for the youth she lost so quickly. She needed the security of Joe's body close knowing if he had been alive she could not have brought him here. The sky had started to lighten before she fell into a fitful sleep.

Charlie all six foot four of him talking to the desk clerk turned and smiled his father's smile when his mother said his name. Adelia loved Charlie's smile. Seeing it here this morning frightened her. Maybe she only thought Charlie had his father's smile. Maybe she did not remember. Relieved Jane was not with her son Adelia enjoyed the security of his taking her arm and leading her to his waiting car.

"You look different mom," he said as he put her in the passenger side. She wanted to ask if the thirty pounds lost from her waist and hips, the soft brown that covered her gray hair, the caps that erased the gap in her front teeth made her prettier. She wanted to show Charlie the new cloths she purchased for this visit and ask it they flattered her. She didn't. She could not let Charlie know how important it was to her to look pretty here.

The drive took them along a strip of lakeshore on the east side of Lake West Okoboji. Charlie pointed out homes of friends and the small local airport before parking in front of a cement block building painted light green. A sign outside said 'O'Farrells'. Inside waiting to order pancakes Adelia studied friendly faces and smiling eyes. Her emotions conflicted between wanting to see a familiar face yet fearful of what would happen if she did. The pancakes, feather light, came with hot syrup and slabs of butter. She ate two. Charlie ate five. He asked three men sitting with coffee cups at a long narrow table about their fishing. They complained it wasn't good now that the rich kids from Des Moines and Omaha were out in their personal watercraft.

They enjoyed a second cup of coffee before Charlie ushered her out again thanking her for coming. Her response was to question his decision to open a law practice in Okoboji.

"Mom, I felt a kinship with this area the first time I came."

" I wanted you to settle in Virginia. The winters are easier and there are more opportunities."

"I knew that mom. I planned to stay in Virginia before Jane and I had made the thirty hours drive here from Charlottesville. We got out of the car, looked at the lake and I felt I had come home. It was like a part of me had always been here."

Adelia let out a strange sound. Charlie looked at her in surprise. Adelia cringed, took a deep breath, and then was silent as Charlie saw her retreat inside herself.

They drove silently along the lake shore Charlie pointing out the Haywards Bay cottage where she would move the end of the week. It sat on a deep lot. Burr oak trees shading it with beautiful arches too numerous to count. A sign on it back porch said 'Tennessee.'

About a mile later Charlie pulled into a small house across the road from the lake. "My house," he announced, "I'm proud to show it to my mother."

Inside it smelled musty. Adelia noticed a spider weaving a web near the ceiling of the small back entry. She said nothing as Charlie proudly showed her the kitchen, the living room with a field stone fireplace, the small sunroom with a lake view and a large room family room off the kitchen. Upstairs three doors opened off a hall, one to the master bedroom, the second to a bath. The third filled with boxes and books appeared to have once been a second bedroom. The geometric patterns on the wallpaper suggested it had been hung in the early sixties.

Adelia asked to use the bathroom. She locked the door before turning on the cold-water faucet to cover the sound of her opening drawers and cupboards with little guilt. She found two men's electric razors, a package of men's disposable razors, two can of shaving crème, three kinds of after shave, Brut deodorant, several spent bars of soap, shampoo and a few miss-matched towels, toilet paper, and face tissue. No toilet articles of a young woman. Jane either was not living in the house or had taken her things out before Adelia arrived.

Adelia envious at the thought of Jane sleeping with her son recognized all young people lived together before marriage now. Adelia did not approve but found cleansing in that fact. The tour of Charlie's house over they continued the drive north around the lake.

"We'll pick Jane up at her parents house. She is living there until the wedding," Charlie related.

"Oh not with you?"

"Mom, you sound surprised."

"Well." Adelia had surprised herself with her question and her reaction.

Charlie did not wait for her to say more, "Mom, I feel strange telling you this. Jane and I don't live together. In fact we have never had sex." Charlie's face reddened but he hurried on. "Jane decided in junior high she would not have sex before marriage. Her best friend got pregnant. She saw the friend's grief and decided to save herself for marriage. She has and we both lust for our wedding night. I wasn't so pure. I need not tell you. You were the one who found the half-used packages of rubbers in the glove compartment of my convertible my junior year of high school."

They drove silently for several blocks Adelia surprised by what she had heard but too embarrassed to comment. Sex was a subject she had never discussed with her son. She never discussed sex with anyone except a little bit with Mary Claire. It wasn't proper. It happened with Joe, but they didn't talk about it.

Charlie had to be aware of her embarrassment but continued to talk. "Mom you and dad set my moral code. I was in sixth grade Steve was my best friend. We were playing at Tom Jacob's house. Steve's dad came over and he and Tom's mother locked themselves in an upstairs

18

bedroom. Tom said he didn't like Steve's dad fucking his mother. We didn't really know what fucking was exactly but Tom and Steve were upset. And in the next few years many of my friends' parents were getting divorces or sleeping around. One-day dad and I were fishing off the pier at Lake Tahoe. I asked him if he slept with other women. He gave me a firm 'no.' He said he was true to you and his marriage vows. Dad coughed and sputtered but he told me sex only belonged in marriage and I need remember that. There was a fish on my hook then. He tried to help me reel it in but we lost it. We never talked about sex again."

"He was a wonderful man."

"Yea and that talk gave me pride. My friends talked about their parents, extra-martial sexual activities I felt superior to them. Like I had a greater responsibility to make something out of my self. I only wish he could have been my dad when he was younger."

Adelia did not respond. Charlie had turned the car up to a two story old frame house off the lake. A girl bearing a striking resemblance to Jane stood pouring potting soil in huge clay pots. Adelia got out of the car and slammed the door hard before Charlie introduced her to Susie, Jane's younger sister. Susie led them in the back door of the house to a kitchen cluttered with the doohickey of a large family and smelling of fresh coffee and cinnamon and cluttered with pictures of family, Jane, the middle child, and her two older brothers and two younger sisters.

CHAPTER IV

There were the days I sat under a tree watching the other girls and boys recording their faces in my memory yet they knew not that I existed at all. **BUG**

Adelia recognized Elizabeth as soon as she saw her standing near the oven pulling out a pan of sweet smelling oatmeal raisin cookies as the chimes of a clock in a far off room started to announce the eleventh hour. The years had put extra pounds on Elizabeth's figure. Elizabeth turned smiled at Charlie showing the nicotine stains on once perfect white teeth. Elizabeth coughed, the raspy cough of a middle-aged woman who started smoking in her teens and never quit.

Did Elizabeth still smoke Salems? A thin Elizabeth with dark curls and clear brown eyes had. She also drove a mahogany plank Century Arabian pulling boys on water skis and smiled at her reflection in the mirror in the bathroom at the Roof Garden.

Elizabeth gave Adelia cigarettes. Adelia felt grown up smoking. In Joe's house the only rule, *No Smokers*. His first wife died of lung cancer. At first Adelia hated the rule. She smoked in the bathroom on her fifth day in his house. Joe told her if she did it again she was gone. She was angry but did not smoke again. Today she could not tolerate smoking. Elizabeth coughed again, the cough raspy and deep. Catching her breath, she offered fresh coffee in heavy white mugs with 'IT'S A BEAUTIFUL OKOBOJI MORNING' in blue cursive fired on the mug. The coffee strong and hot tasted good. Adelia and Charlie each took a big oatmeal and raisin cookie never confessing they had breakfasted on buttermilk pancakes.

Sitting at the big round oak table on mismatched chairs, Charlie, and Adelia listened to Elizabeth out line plans for the August wedding and Adelia's social schedule in the weeks before. Refilling Adelia's coffee cup Elizabeth said, "you remind me of someone I once knew whose name I'm trying to remember."

Adelia took another sip of coffee and said nothing praying her face did not reveal her emotions.

Jane arrived in the kitchen then covered in a sparkling white terry bathrobe her hair wet from the shower. Charlie had seen her first standing in the doorway and a smile had crossed his face. Adelia had not seen her since the late night call from Charlie telling Adelia he and Jane would marry. Looking at Jane poised, confident, smiling, beautiful Adelia's dislike for the girl grew. Charlie's slate blue eyes followed Jane's every move. He adored the girl. Charlie's father once looked at Adelia that way. It was a memory she would always carry. Adelia was lost in her own thoughts when Elizabeth directed a question to her "Is this the first time you have traveled to Iowa?"

Charlie saved her from answering, "I tried to get mother to Iowa when I was ten. We were driving cross-county in a new Buick ranch wagon. Dad had a meeting. I was intent on visiting all the state Capitols. Had a scrapbook of pictures of me standing in front of the Capitols of a twenty-two states. I planned a route home to take us through Des Moines, Iowa. "Mom said we had to go another way," Charlie continued. "She was not interested in seeing Des Moines, Iowa. It was unlike her; I nearly always got my way, the spoiled only child."

Charlie smiled and everybody laughed but Adelia before he went on. "I begged but still she said no. We drove from Omaha to Kansas City, Missouri and missed the Capitol in Des Moines. I had a tantrum. Still, mom did not give in."

"We are glad she is here now," Elizabeth interjected.

"Believe me it was not easy," Charlie replied looking straight at his mother who refused to let her eyes meet his.

Elizabeth started talking, "We Iowans are our own people. Most of us have deep roots in the state." She rambled on, " My children are descendants of pioneer families who settled from the Mississippi to the

Missouri Rivers. Irish, German, mixed with a bit of English and French. None came directly from Europe. They had settled first in the Atlantic states. The Irish came to escape discriminations in the east. The rest looking for homes on the fertile prairie."

"Mother, don't bore her," Jane interrupted seemingly impatient with her mother's attempt to trace the family tree.

"I find it interesting Jane." Adelia felt sorry for Elizabeth. Her perfect daughter had been rude.

"Mrs. Hogan we are going to show you how beautiful this area is and make you feel at home," Jane said ignoring the tension between she and her mother.

Adelia tried but no smile appeared on her face. Charlie's look told her he sensed her feelings and did not like them.

CHAPTER V

August 1963

Grandmother,

I do not want to upset you but I no longer have a calling to join the Franciscan sisters. Yesterday Chip took me to Crandall's Lodge, a three-story frame structure with screened porches and a big dinning room with many round oak tables. We ate second helpings of pork roast and mashed potatoes and green beans picked from the garden. The lemonade was fresh squeezed and there was tart rhubarb crisp with homemade vanilla ice cream for desert. Later we sat on the sand beach in front looking south over the wide expanse of Spirit Lake and talked about our wedding. It will be on the lakeshore. Rex will wear flowers on his collar.

Love, Bug

With Jane in the back seat and Adelia in the front Charlie drove north and started around Spirit Lake. Jane explained Spirit Lake Iowa's largest natural lake touched the Minnesota border. As they drove around the north end of the lake Adelia suggested, they stop for lunch at Crandall's Lodge. "Crandall's?" Charlie's voice registered confusion.

"A brochure at the New Inn mentioned there was a Crandall's Lodge on the north end of Spirit Lake," Adelia lied.

"Never heard of it but I'll ask." Charlie stopped and rolled down the window near a gray haired lady in a red windbreaker walking two collies. He asked for directions to Crandall's Lodge.

"Tore it down at least fifteen years ago. A piety, it was a landmark and an unusual place to eat. The owners served fresh garden vegetables from their own garden. But you know those developers." She shook her head.

Charlie thanked her. Adelia quickly commented the brochure must have been old. Jane said it was strange the New Inn would have a brochure fifteen years old.

At the end of the week the new dark green Oldsmobile Bravada Adelia ordered from a Spencer dealer was delivered. Her wedding gift for Charlie and Jane she would use it while she was in Iowa and then it would be theirs. The next day she moved into Tennessee. Nobody seemed to know why the cottage set on the deep lot on Haywards Bay had been named Tennessee but thought maybe one of its early owners was from there and the name had not been changed.

Shaded by the lush green leaves of Burr Oaks whose roots found moisture deep in the banks surrounding the lake the rectangular one story cottage had to be a century old. There was a sweeping screened front porch, three bedrooms, one bath and a stone fireplace, and a back-screened porch just off the kitchen. Adelia chose the back bedroom with the king sized feather bed for hers. She opened the windows. A playful lake breeze teased the curtain. She stood savoring sweet lake air and for the second time in a week feeling a spark inside her ignite and fear gripping her person. Later she pulled herself together and drove to the grocery store.

There she purchased red apples, green grapes, bananas, a small cantaloupe, fresh ground coffee, skim milk, a paper carton of orange juice, two pounds of sugar, a package of ten little cereal boxes and beer and wine. Driving back to Tennessee she stopped at a small restaurant with a deck over looking Lake Minnawashta a small lake south and east of West Okoboji. She ordered wine. They had only beer so she settled for a bottle of Budweiser light and sipped it slowly while watching a muscular young man skiing behind a yellow and white ski boat. Some one at a near table commented his name was Murphy and he was one of the best water skiers on the lake. Adelia recalled the day before Charlie left for his freshman year at the University of Virginia. Joe sat close to her on their pier that extended into Lake Tahoe on Camellia Bay. They were watching Charlie in a wet suit trying to ski behind a friend's boat.

Charlie, not well coordinated, struggled for an hour before he finally made a complete sweep in the bay and fell down.

The next morning they drove to Reno and put Charlie and his trunks on an Amtrak train headed east. There were tears in both their eyes as they drove back up Mount Rose toward their home on Lake Tahoe that they were to sell the next year. It was deadly silent on their return. They woke early the next morning. They shared an intimacy reserved for marriage partners long faithful to each other with an understanding of each other's limitations and needs. While they lay close a soft morning breeze teased their curtains and a chorus of birds welcomed sunrise. Their naked bodies touching Joe said, "I have never forgiven myself for having you outside our marriage vows."

Adelia kissed him gently on the forehead. "You were not to blame." Her thoughts went to the man who once brought excitement to her life.

Joe pulled her close and told her of his love and she told him of her love for him. She would never confess she planned the night he first had her. He would never know how repulsive the act she positioned herself for had been that night or that she felt she was a prostitute. Nor did she tell him in the early years she was with him because of need and that there had once been a special love she could not have. Joe loved her from the beginning and had slowly shown her the reward that came from returning his love. Each day with Joe she found more contentment but never excitement.

Joe spoke then slowly, deliberately, "I know I never gave you the excitement a younger man, one closer to your own age would have given you." After he spoke he gently fingered the silver bracelet she always wore on her left wrist. She felt shame. He never asked where the bracelet came from or why she wore it. She never shared its history with him.

She waited until he looked in her eyes. "Joe," she spoke tenderly, "you gave me so much."

"But Adelia I know it mattered to you that I was over twenty-five years your senior. I wish I could make you understand no man could have been as lucky as I to have you and Charlie. You my dear will soon inherit my money. Never question but you have earned it."

"Joe," she started to talk.

"Just don't let another man spend it for you. It is yours and Charlie's."

CHAPTER VI

***All nature without voice or sound, Christopher
Smart 1722-1771
Canadian geese, the pair glides silently
bodies shadowed by the morning sun
one with the water
they float in solitude
nary a ripple nor a wake.
Where have they come from?
Why are they here?
Their silence,
their mystery,
their presence
part of the secrets of
nature that tantalize me but
never reveal the unknown
force that brought the geese to the lake.

Adelia Hogan

Honking geese flying overhead woke her. A cool breeze tickled Adelia's shoulders. She pulled the down comforter around her body and snuggled into the feather bed enjoying the euphoric security as she listened to a medley of birds' voices. The high staccato of the songbirds now and then was interrupted by the harsh caw of a crow.

In the kitchen at the east end of the house glints of sunlight gold crept in the window. Adelia poured a glass of orange juice from a paper carton and took it to the front porch. Mellow sunrays played in the oak leaves. The juice untouched she stared at the lush green of the trees, such peace and beauty. Retrieving a lined notebook from her train case she attempted to record the morning in words of poetry. Depressed the words came slowly. Finally she put her pencil down. Her soul hungry for prayer, her body was not able to shake the depression.

Adelia dressed then in a khaki skirt and light blue short sleeved Polo shirt. She would lunch at one with Elizabeth. At seven there was a dinner party a friend of Elizabeth was giving. The hours before one would pass slowly. Putting on walking shoes she started south. For a time she walked between the lake and the lake shore homes before cutting across someone's lawn and heading back north on the road. A young man driving a truck loaded with dock building materials, a mother with teenagers in a red Jeep, a young woman in a blue pick up and a suited man in a shinny Chevrolet Suburban passed her. Every driver waved. She returned their greetings. It seemed here everybody thought they knew you. If they didn't, they wanted to know who you were, where you came from and what you were doing here. The friendliness was comforting, yet intrusive. A small dog barked then followed her. Somewhere on the beach someone practiced scales on a piano, the sound of deliberately pushed keys breaking the stillness.

Back at Tennessee the dog watched Adelia rock in a big wicker rocker on the front porch listening to the wind tease the oak leaves. Finally the dog shook and headed off. An on coming motorboat broke the near silence. A boy and a girl sat close in the boat its wake creating a blemish on the mirror smooth lake. Adelia sought to chase away returning memories.

At a few minutes before one o'clock Adelia drove to the Central Emporium, a collection of shops and eateries located on the south east shore of Lake West Okoboji in the town of Arnolds Park. The building once a busy dance hall now housed vendors selling shirts, swimming suits, sunglasses, candy and souvenirs. On the lake side with big plate glass windows over looking the lake was Maxwell's Restaurant where Elizabeth had reserved a window table. The hostess called Elizabeth by name, as did the slender red headed waitress who came to ask about drinks and promptly returned with two wine glasses of chardonnay and patiently waited while they scanned the menu before ordering salads.

Adelia envied Elizabeth's ease and familiarity in the surroundings. "You are known here," Adelia commented.

"My children are. When you have five, you spend your adult life as somebody's mom. The employees here are their friends."

"Elizabeth I'm glad we have this time alone." Adelia wanted to enlist her support in getting Charlie and Jane to return to Charlottesville.

Elizabeth broached a different subject. She spoke quietly. "The money is appreciated."

"The least," Adelia began but was interrupted.

Elizabeth spoke quickly like she didn't want to say it but knew it needed to be said. "Your check saved the day. Andrew won't say thank you. He is a proud man. Doesn't like charity from anyone but most particularly not from a woman. It has been difficult raising and educating five children on his salary and mine. The Iowa public schools are among the best in the nation but as English and Science teachers we are not paid well. One of us should have gone into public school administration where the salaries are the highest. But we both had this idea we should teach not run the school and take attendance."

"I," Adelia attempted to interject but again Elizabeth stopped her. "It was not that way for me growing up. My father was a physician in Des Moines." Adelia saw the pride surface as Elizabeth continued. "There was always money. Andrew grew up poor. He feels he never met my family's expectations."

"You need not"

But Elizabeth intended to continue, "My father spent all of his money, died before doctors had been covered very long by social security. My mother barely survived. She is dead now. I don't care about the wedding for my self but I care for my daughter."

Charlie had suggested Adelia send the money saying it was not for Jane but for Jane's mother. It didn't matter really. Adelia could never spend all the money Joe left her. She thought of the Elizabeth she studied from afar decades earlier and the strange twists their lives had taken. Then Adelia earned $30 a week as a summer girl plus a ticket on the Greyhound from and to her home. Adelia had Joe's generosity and benefited from his quiet way of seeing that she and Charlie always had more than they needed or wanted. Joe may have been boring yet he was humble and never flaunting. She must be the same way.

CHAPTER VII

Everybody likes the middle child.
The middle child does not get the privileges of the older nor the concessions of the younger. Unknown

The red headed waitress brought their salads, crisp greens, cucumbers, tomatoes, feta cheese, Greek olives dressed with spicy olive oil and vinegar. The first bite was delicious yet Adelia picked at hers. In her emotional turmoil she had lost her appetite.

By the time the women finished with lunch Elizabeth detailed the wedding at the church and the reception. Adelia had been told were to sit, stand and pray. Elizabeth, the schoolteacher, gave orders like a general. Her orders delivered she called for coffee and lit a cigarette. "You are lucky you don't smoke." Elizabeth coughed as she talked. "Did you ever?"

"Years ago."

"I wish I could remember whom you remind me of." Adelia feeling her face tighten was relieved Elizabeth continued, "I shouldn't say this but Jane feels you don't like her."

"Oh but I do." Shaken by the confrontation Adelia hoped her voice did not betray her feelings.

"I told her that. Everyone likes Jane."

"I understand." Again Adelia lied. She didn't understand. She didn't want to understand. Elizabeth's daughter was taking her son and had brought her and Charlie to this place they should not be. She was unhappy with her son for loving Jane and hated Jane for loving him.

33

The waitress came with the check. Elizabeth smiled and said thank you but did not resist Adelia handing the girl a crisp bill and saying she did not need change. The girl pleased with the generosity of Adelia's tip gave her a special thank you.

Adelia excused herself while Elizabeth talked to the hostess. Jealously revered in Adelia's body as it had the day she met Jane and her life started to fall apart. That day Charlie still a student at the University of Virginia was celebrating his twenty-sixth birthday. Adelia and Joe had flown to Dulles International Airport, rented a Lincoln Town car and drove two hours east past Culpeper into the rolling Virginia countryside. They arrived at the Boar head's Lodge outside Charlottesville just before five in the afternoon. Joe called Charlie at his fraternity house to confirm their seven o'clock dinner reservations at a restaurant in the Barrack's Mall. They were surprised to see Charlie come in with a blond haired girl at his side.

"Mom and Dad this is Jane Abbott. I asked her to join us." He introduced her tenderly.

Joe, in his quiet boring way, charmed Jane, made her welcome as Adelia focused attention on Charlie. Joe ordered wine and toasted the occasion and Jane while the waitress returned for their food order. They finished coffee and chocolate cheesecake, that Charlie claimed was his favorite birthday cake before Joe asked, "Jane please tell me where you are from?"

"Iowa. I grew up in Iowa." She seemed apologetic.

"She grew up on a lake," Charlie felt the need to give her proper credentials.

Adelia did not want to hear more but Joe pursued, "What was the name of the lake?"

"West Okoboji. It is in the northwest corner of the state."

"A deep blue water lake close to Minnesota and South Dakota," Joe volunteered proud of his knowledge of geography. "Pretty area?"

"To me it is one of the beautiful spots in the world. Although I should be frank and admit I have done little traveling. But I generally don't talk about Iowa here. In the east they flinch if you say you are from Iowa."

"People on both coasts are ignorant about the beauty and culture of the Midwest," Joe interjected.

"Yes and if they comment about Boise or potatoes or ask how far I live from Cleveland it is easier to smile and say nothing."

Adelia excused herself. Locked in a stall in the woman's restroom she tried to stop her hands from shaking. She started hating Jane for the anguish the girl was causing her, hate the only way that Adelia could counter act the threat Jane brought to the essence of her existence.

CHAPTER VIII

Jefferson's school, the grounds, the lawn
the old buildings preserved,
the new buildings segregated
under blue skies
that often fill
with low black clouds.
Though lightening strikes and
rain laces the air with humidity
life continues for the young and old
who find a solace in the university,
the heart of Charlottesville

ADELIA HOGAN

Adelia and Joe spent six weeks in Charlottesville. They had planned to be there six days. The day after Charlie's birthday they drove their rental car up the mountain to the entrance to the grounds of Jefferson's home. There they took a small bus up the mountain to Monticello. Joe recited history all the way. As always, boring Adelia.

Entering Jefferson's house they followed with a group the tour leader, a woman who wore a blue pillbox hat and spoke with a strange accent. Slowly she described the holes cut in the floor for the weights of Jefferson's clock, a circle eight mechanism that opened the front door. She pointed out the silent butler in the dining room and a small bed in the alcove. She twice explained Jefferson's invention that allowed him to make copies of his handwriting.

The sun bright, Joe and Adelia elected to skip the bus ride down the mountain and walk past the vegetable garden and the area where the one hundred or more slaves, today a stain on Jefferson's record, had lived in shanties. They walked slowly on a blacktopped path past a cemetery and through the forest. The next day they strolled the mall in downtown Charlottesville and ate at the Hardware Store restaurant where the condiments were delivered to the table in toolboxes. On day three they drove to Mitchie Tavern and that evening to Madison's home. There they sat outside and listed to the opera sung in English and shared a box lunch before a thunderstorm cut the evening short. On the way back to the Bore head Adelia told Joe she wanted to retire in Charlottesville. Joe said that would be fine and Adelia would always have all the money she would ever need. Neither said anything for several miles and then it was as though he were lecturing, "Adelia there is a lot of money. It is your pay for the years of happiness you have given this aging fossil. There are no strings. It is yours. Only one caveat do not take a man that falls for your money. You are a giver. Don't let a taker take advantage." She did not respond.

In between their jaunts Charlie and Jane joined Joe and Adelia for dinners at the Virginian, The Tavern, Sackett's. Never did Adelia carry on a conversation with Jane. She talked to her son and Joe with Jane.

Adelia fell in love with Charlottesville, the university, the mountains and the closeness to Washington, D.C. On the last day of their scheduled visit she and Joe drove through the clouds on Skyline Drive in the Blue ridge Mountains returning to Charlottesville after the sun set. Adelia in a long ivory nightgown was brushing her hair. Joe came behind, stroked her face and asked in his gentle way, "What is it you don't like about Jane?"

"I like Jane," Adelia blurted out.

"Don't pretend darling. I have been with you too many years for you to fool me that easily. Adelia you have judged her too quickly."

"She"

He did not let her speak, "She likes your son, probably loves him, and from the sparkle in his eyes when he looks at her he is hooked. It is normal for you to be jealous."

"I," Adelia started but didn't know what to say. In all their years together Joe had only once criticized her and that was when she was smoking cigarettes. Never for anything else and now she didn't know how to respond except with anger.

She did not respond before he continued, "There have been other girls and"

"I have treated them better."

"You have treated them very well my dear that is why I do not understand this."

"Maybe"

"Adelia, Jane is smart, kind, will soon have a degree. She is a Midwesterner with solid family roots."

"And I should like her for that?" Adelia surprised even herself with her reply.

"If Jane is the one Charlie chooses and you alienate her you may lose Charlie." Joe hesitated then before adding in a strange way "And you will need them both."

She didn't understand then what he was saying. Anxious to close the conversation she suggested they go to bed.

Joe gently squeezed her arm. He seemed to know it was the end of her talking about Jane but as they were falling asleep he asked, "What is it with Iowa?"

She said nothing only shut her eyes never knowing how many time this conversation would ring in her head, remembering Joe had tried to prepare her for what was to soon come.

The next morning carrying luggage to the rental car Joe had his first heart attack. He spent five weeks at the University of Virginia Medical Center and another week at the Boarshead before he was ready to return to Chicago. Two years later he was dead.

C H A P T E R   I X

discover a true friend and find gold
true friends are scarcer than precious metals
as does the gold the friend shines
never have I found a true friend
I wanted to let go

ADEALI HOGAN

Kittie Carlson said she lived in the Colonial farmhouse facing south on Haywards Bay when she called Adelia to confirm the supper invitation Elizabeth had extended. "It is a lady's only night," Kittie volunteered. Adelia assured her she would be there.

Adelia elected to walk the less than two blocks from Tennessee. Several guests were gathered when she entered the two-story living room and Kittie quickly introduced her to the group. Some faces looked familiar to Adelia. She enviously recognized she was among long time women friends.

Kittie served a fine Chardonnay in Waterford wine glasses. Adelia took hers to the brick patio on the lakeside of the house. Alone she stared out at the water darkening as the sun slipped down the western horizon. The sun had nearly descended when a woman to whom she had not been introduced joined her.

The woman looked at the lake before confronting Adelia with, "You are Charlie's mother. Elizabeth said you were coming and we should meet. We are the widows, the bunch of old, single females, that the married ones assume belong together."

"Here there are no secrets," Adelia said quietly before she looked to the lake.The woman heard her and laughed. Adelia hesitated before laughing too. It felt good to laugh. It had been a long time since she had.

"I'm Eleanor Windsor," the woman continued. "I hate the name Eleanor; try to get my friends to call me Ellie."

"I'm Adelia Hogan."

"I know. I'm hoping you will have lunch with me tomorrow."

"Tomorrow I", Adelia had nothing planned. The invitation had come quickly.

"You can't say no. Elizabeth told me to ask you, she said you had nothing planned."

"You don't have"

"Don't have to follow Elizabeth's orders," Ellie interjected, "I generally do. She does not like it if I don't. Elizabeth suffers from the general syndrome, the result of managing her five children and teaching school. Yet she has done well by a lot of people.

"You know her well," Adelia interjected.

"This group all grew up together, spending the long beautiful summers of youth on this lake. We come back summers thinking we'll find the magic of our childhood. Sometimes we do just a bit." Ellie paused then turned toward the lake, a look of melancholy crossing her face. She looked silently and then continued, "Elizabeth married a local boy and made this her full time home. The rest of us live under better financial circumstances than Elizabeth. We inherited well. Elizabeth's father spent all of his money on a mistress although she has never admitted that. She and Andrew have done dam well with their kids."

Adelia found Ellie's honesty refreshing but was curious about the mistress. She was ready to accept Ellie's invitation as Elizabeth joined them. "Kittie sent me out to smoke." She coughed and lit her cigarette. "She forgets the days we all smoked. I'm banished because I'm the only one who still does."

"And we want you to quit," Ellie said softly. "We make it hard for you to smoke because we love you."

"Enough," Elizabeth cut her off and turned to Adelia. "You and Eleanor will have a good time at lunch tomorrow. What time is she picking you up?"

Ellie winked at Adelia. Adelia smiled. Had she not taken an immediate liking to Ellie she would have instantly rebelled.

"I'm older than Elizabeth that is why she calls me Eleanor."

Ellie laughed again. Elizabeth didn't see the humor. Inside some one had turned on the tape player and the sweet music of the Beach Boys drifted outside.

"I love that music," Ellie said. I remember the night the Beach Boys played at the roof garden. I feel in love with all of them.

Adelia wanted to say that every time she head a Beach Boys song played she thought of her first love and how they had enjoyed their first Beach Boy concert together. Joe knew how she enjoyed the Beach Boys music and as a birthday surprise one year her took her to one of their concerts. She had thanked him for the gift but never told her how it brought back memories she could not forget.

CHAPTER X

The catch of the day was grilled yellow fin tuna advertised as fresh. If it wasn't fresh, it was as good as fresh. Seasoned with lime and fresh cracked pepper and served with a crisp garden salad and hot sour dough bread Adelia savored it all. She and Ellie extended lunch with conversation. By the time the waitress brought the check Ellie knew more about Adelia's life than she should have told.

Adelia also learned Ellie, who had homes on Dixon Beach on West Okoboji and on Grand Avenue in Des Moines was the granddaughter of a former governor of Iowa. Her family controlled Standard Insurance a company that owned three of the largest buildings in downtown Des Moines. Mick Windsor whose father ran a yard service out of Arnold's Park married her for her money. Ellie said after two children Mick asked for a divorce and alimony. He planned to marry a girl ten years younger. He was killed. Drunk he ran her new Cadillac into a light pole two days after he filed for divorce. "Thank goodness a policeman saw it happen," Ellie volunteered, "I would have been accused of orchestrating it."

"Oh, why?"

"There was a million-dollar life insurance policy my grandfather had purchased on Mick's life. I was the beneficiary. Then six months later my grandfather died and with the multimillion dollar trust fund set up in his will I was assured a life free of financial worries."

"Financial security rarely comes easily," Adelia remarked thinking of praying for a little bit of money, not her soul and remembering Joe's caveat not to let a man marry her for her money.

Finally the proprietor of the restaurant locked the front door. The women not ready to close their conversation Ellie suggested, they have coffee at Broadway Brew a yellow, red, purple and green coffee house on Broadway the short street that ran through the business district of old town Arnolds Park. There they ordered espressos made from fresh ground beans and sat out side on the porch watching traffic on the street and boats on the lake. The owner, Katie, an attractive young woman with a contagious smile stopped by their table and exchanged greetings with Ellie who introduced her to Adelia. Adelia liked Katie immediately.

That day Ellie asked Adelia if she would accompany her to Lakeview Nursing home. Ellie went to the home several days each week to read poetry to the residents and treat them to chocolate truffles she bought at a local handmade candy shop.

Adelia anxious to spend more time with Ellie said she would go then thinking of her discomfort in nursing homes immediately regretted it.

CHAPTER XI

Adelia first met her grandmother's sister Catherine Dailey in Longview Nursing Home. Catherine was Adelia's only living relative besides Charlie and Joe. Catherine had no one else and the home found Adelia when Catherine grew senile. Adelia's father died just before her third birthday. There was always a picture of him on the buffet in the dinning room of the apartment where she lived with her mother and grandmother. They asked Adelia if she remembered him, she said she did but mostly it was a lie. If she did remember him the father in her mind did not look like the man in the picture. Photographs of dead people were strange things. Like you sort of knew what the person looked like but you were not exactly sure and maybe sometimes you were better just hearing about them and thinking what they looked like instead of remembering them from a picture.

Adelia's mother fell off the balcony of their apartment and died. Adelia was nine. Girls in the neighborhood said she jumped. Adelia never let herself believe that it was anything but a fall against a loose railing. Mary Claire said it was a fall and Mary Claire became her best friend. Adelia's grandmother died when Adelia was five days past her eighteenth birthday. She had pictures of her mother and her grandmother in her head.

Longview's call telling Adelia she had a great-aunt at the home met resistance. She had no picture of Aunt Catherine and no memory she had ever been told the woman existed. Joe insisted Adelia go see her. He said she needed relatives. They went and the place smelled of disinfectant and urine and old age. The carpet was orange and the furniture was dark and heavy.

Catherine lived a year. Joe took Adelia there every Sunday and Adelia tried to make conversation with a woman she had never known and who forget she had been there as soon as she left. Every week Joe suggested Charlie go with them. He told Adelia seeing others grow older prepared you for growing old. Every week Adelia rejected Joe's suggestion. She wanted to protect Charlie. She refused to face the reality Charlie was being raised by a man older than many of the residents at Longview. Joe arranged Catherine's funeral. Nobody was there except an aid from the home, Adelia and Joe. Joe said Charlie needed to be there that he needed to know about funerals before someone close to him died. Adelia grew angry. Joe let it drop.

Adelia decided when she went back to Longview to pick up the few things Catherine left in life washed and packed in a shabby suitcase she would never go to a nursing home again. It took her a long time to go through the suitcase. Ultimately she did and found the letters, twenty-five in a tattered stationary box. Adelia wasn't certain if she had recognized the postmark or the handwriting first. The letters were addressed to her at her grandmother's apartment and had been opened. Reading them tears came and years melted. Adelia never knew how they got in Aunt Catherine Dailey's stationary box or why they had never been delivered to her. She thought of writing back but too many years had passed. Now the letters and one of hers to Charlie were in her blue Samsonite train case, the piece of luggage her grandmother gave her just before she died acquired by redeeming thirty books of Green stamps given at the grocery and drug stores and saved and carefully pasted in the books. Adelia thought her Grandmother was saving the stamps for sheets for her own bed. She was so surprised to get the train case she hugged and kissed her Grandmother. Adelia had never shown her Grandmother such affection. Not many days later she found her Grandmother dead in her bed between worn sheets. Adelia cried for days. That she had hugged and kissed her grandmother gave her some solace. She decided then the blue Samsonite train case would never be far from her sight.

Only when Adelia was dead could Charlie read the letters, poems, and diary she kept in that case. Once he tried to look in her train case. Her fear he would see what was there had released anger. It was the one time she yelled at her son. He could not know during her lifetime the many secrets of her life recorded there.

CHAPTER XII

The five female residents in the lounge, cloths hanging from frail withered frames, eyes glazed, sat raising hands and feet in slow awkward motions to the command of a young woman with dirty hair, a double chin and fleshy arms dressed in gray sweat pants and a T shirt with LAKEVIEW EXERCISE CLUB in bright red letters on the front.

Watching the ladies struggle with the simple task saddened Adelia. Would Charlie and Jane put her here someday and visit with her on Sunday afternoons?

The exercise class over three of the women shuffled off. The remaining two women were joined by three withered men. A girl in a pink uniform with blond hair black at the roots pushed a woman in a wheel chair towards them. The woman in the wheel chair raised her head looking directly at Adelia. Something in the woman's face caused Adelia to smile. The woman returned the smile. Her slate blue eyes more alert than most of the other residents were sadder too as if she understood but did not accept that she was put here to die.

Ellie stood in front of the group and read a poem about summer. As she slowly said each word all attention focused on her. In her melodic voice she spoke of warmth, beauty and hope; sunshine and laughter; love and life; joy and sunshine. The residents smiled yet in this place there was little hope and no sunshine. Ellie read so well Adelia wanted to ask that she read one of the poems she had hidden in her blue train case.

Ellie finished a poem describing the beauty of sunsets before passing truffles. She patiently waited as each resident made the laborious decision of whether to take raspberry or French silk.

Adelia cautiously approached the woman in the wheel chair. The woman extended a bony hand, "I'm Agnes Luc."

Startled Adelia hesitated before taking the extended hand. "I'm Adelia Hogan."

"Have not seen you here before?"

"I live in Chicago."

"What brings you here?"

"My son's wedding."

"Is he from here?"

"Now he is. He is marrying a girl from Okoboji."

"Boys are like that they go with the girl's family."

Adelia caught sadness in the woman's voice. She knew before she asked the woman that she had a son and she knew his name.

Adelia asked, "Your son"

The woman interrupted and said his name.

Hearing his name Adelia's hands shook.

Mrs. Luc noticed. "What is the matter my dear?"

"Nothing."

"I sense something but I shan't pry."

Adelia did not understand why she confided in Agnes, shared her sorrow in losing Joe, and her inability to celebrate with joy the forth coming wedding of her son.

"I did not celebrate my son's wedding with joy. I have been the one to suffer. I have a good boy yet my daughter-in-law does all she can to keep me apart from him."

"You don't like her?" Adelia should not have asked. It was wrong to pry.

Agnes didn't answer her question. She only said, "I never saw the excitement in my son he should have had as a young bridegroom. I thought he loved someone else. I never knew who."

The words cut into Adelia's heart. "Do they live far away?" She had to know.

"Only five miles but it as well be a thousand. They once lived in my family cottage on Des Moines Beach. He spent all the money he inherited from his father for new windows, siding, plumbing, wiring, paint, expensive wallpaper, furniture and carpet. Turned it into a show place for her. She never thought it was good enough. It hurt him. They had to sell it. Needed the money, she over spent. They no longer could afford the house. They don't think I know that. It wasn't him. He is frugal but her. She spends." Agnes stopped herself, "I sound bitter. Don't want to, but she never has made my son happy."

Adelia's stomach churned as she listened. She wanted to ask if Agnes had grandchildren but Agnes continued, "If only he had married for love. Like I with his father. My son is good and kind. He deserved such happiness."

Ellie came to tell Adelia she was ready to leave. Adelia squeezed Agnes's hand before quickly following Ellie out into the bright June sunshine.

C H A P T E R   X I I I

Eyes fixed in blank stares
to the distance.
They have run the race
accepted the challenges.
Left with memories
they sit by day
never looking
at those in near by chairs
who with them wait for
the food and the pills
provided with regularity.
Mostly they yearn for the visitor
who may never come.
Experienced, wise.
Hopelessness has replaced
love and laughter and the wish
to share the history that
will die with them.
When I come, I bring a smile.
Sometimes the smile is returned
I see a bit of hope
And I am rewarded.

Eleanor Windsor

The day Adelia met Agnes she volunteered to go to Lakeview with Ellie on her regular visits. Ellie had seemed surprised and asked Adelia why. Adelia told her she thought she could be helpful. Ellie said that was true but wasn't there another reason. Again Adelia said it was only to be helpful refusing to admit to herself or reveal to Ellie anymore.

On those visiting days Ellie read poetry and passed truffles. Adelia and Agnes played cribbage in Agnes' room, a dark place where even at mid day the fluorescent light on the ceiling burned and the tightly made hospital bed, the steel wardrobe and three chairs finished the sterile decor. Agnes unlike her surroundings was warm and compassionate. She talked about her youth, living on the lake, her prized wooden rowboat. Her mother remembering the Queen a boat powered by steam stopping at her dock if a white handkerchief were tied to it. On July and August nights the boat picked up young people who debarked at the Pavilion near the lake on Manhattan Beach. They danced into the night to bands that traveled the Dakotas and Iowa and sometimes the east. Agnes's father was the last signature on her mother's dance card one hot July night. He shyly introduced himself. Studying medicine at the University of Iowa he was visiting a friend's family renting a cottage named Tennessee on Haywards Bay. Agnes said her mother never knew whether he fell in love first with the lake or first with her. He maintained a life long love affair with both. He set up his office in Okoboji rather than take offers in bigger cities. "He often said there is a magic in that lake," Agnes related.

"Magic," Adelia said out loud thinking of the conversation with Ellie on Kittie's porch.

"Yes, magic," Agnes spoke softly, "You discover it as a child. It is harder to find when you are older; but it is there. My father sat tending an old man on his death bed listening to him tell of the spirits in the water and a spell of love placed by an Indian Maiden on the lake Okoboozey. He told my father he forever loved the Indian maiden driven away with her family by the white settlers from this area. He knew he was dying and smiled talking of how their souls would soon meet again on the lake."

"And you believe the dying man's story?" Adelia knowing Agnes did believe it she felt foolish for having asked.

A sad look shadowed Adelia's face. "I do. The old man told my father the magic would live for my father's descendants. Yet my son has lost it."

"There is time for him to find it."

Agnes looking tired replied, "I pray he will."

One morning Adelia arrived at Lakeview as the kitchen help was scraping oatmeal from breakfast bowls to find Agnes sitting in her room with the lights out. Adelia turned the fluorescent tubes on and asked about cribbage. Agnes said no that her mind was too tired to count. Her eyes were dull and her smile had disappeared. She seemed far away as she talked of Helen across the hall whose grandchildren surprised her with a birthday party the day before. Tears formed in Agnes' eyes as she talked about the emptiness in not having grandchildren. She said she had disappointed her father who said the lake carried magic for his children, grand children, and great grandchildren.

Adelia did not try to comfort her but excused herself. In the dark hall way she let her tears flow. She wished she had to courage to rid the woman of her grief. She stayed in the hall a long time before she was ready to return to Agnes's room. Agnes thinking, her tears turned Adelia away apologized. "Thank you for coming back. I am so grateful. You and my memories are all I have."

Adelia notice an album on the bed stand. She inquired about it. Agnes smiled and asked if Adelia wanted to look. Slowly the two women shared pictures of Agnes's son as a baby, a schoolboy and a high school student. Adelia paused at the page covered with his graduation pictures before telling his mother she thought him an incredibly handsome young man.

"He could have had any girl," Agnes said in a voice filled with pride. Adelia nodded her agreement as they quickly scanned pictures of his wedding. He the tall handsome young groom in a white dinner jacket and his bride in a fluffy gown with a train. There were pictures of a six-layer wedding cake, a champagne fountain, and a huge reception, the wedding of Adelia's dreams. Then his chronology stopped. The pictures that followed were older, all in black and white. Adelia asked about one of a young man tall and straight in a white officer's uniform. Agnes said it was her brother. The picture was taken on his last leave home before he was killed on the SS Arizona when Pearl Harbor was bombed. Adelia stared at the small picture haunted by how closely Agnes' son resembled Agnes' brother Agnes puzzled by the time Adelia spent looking at the picture finally interjected, "That bombing was years ago. Few alive remember. The young people today would never understand. Fear and devastation united our country. We couldn't be selfish. Yet wars make no sense. God may let battles be waged so we won't become obsessed with unimportant things."

"Joe was in the war, a fighter pilot."

"What war?"

"The Second World War."

"Oh." Agnes registered surprise. I had not.."

"Had not realized I had married a man old enough to be my father," Adelia cut her off before she felt a need to explain her surprise.

"Did he talk about it?" Agnes inquired anxious to direct the conversation another direction.

"Only once. We sat on the over stuffed sofa in our mammoth living room sipping fine French wine. The sun ready for its late afternoon descent played in the prisms of our cut glass chandelier and rainbow colors soften the interior of the house. Maybe it was the wine. Maybe it was the rainbows of light but he started to recite his story of flying into Pearl Harbor watching the Island being bombed. He was not yet twenty-one at the time but said he saw more horror and destruction in that day than he had ever wanted to know. He said no more, but for the first time I realized memories of the Pear Harbor bombing were the dark shadow he carried."

Agnes looked directly in Adelia's eyes took her hand and her fingers caressed the silver bracelet on Adelia's wrist. "My mother had such a bracelet. My brother sent it to her from Hawaii. She gave it to my son. Told him to give it to his special girl. He did. She was his first girl, a summer romance." Agnes took a breath before saying in a whisper, "I don't think he has ever forgotten her."

Shaken Adelia took a deep breath before removing the bracelet and gently fastening it around the old woman's withered wrist.

"For you."

Agnes fingered the bracelet, "It is like I remember my mother's. Did Joe buy it in Hawaii?"

Adelia did not answer her thoughts reverted to a night under a wide expanse of stars. Seeing Agnes's puzzled look Adelia asked Agnes if she could to see a picture of Agnes's mother.

'I don't have a picture of my mother," Agnes her voice soft responded.

CHAPTER XIV

Ah to sit with a friend
in a comfortable coffee house
sip a cup of fresh brew
and share conversation

Adelia Hogan

Ellie said she had two commandments. First she wore only silk, cotton or wool. "Natural fibers are all that you should have next to your skin," she reasoned. And second she did not trust people that did not have money. "You never understood their true motive for trying to be your friend," she would pronounce. Adelia thought of Ellie as a friend. She could only hope Ellie thought the same of her. Adelia did have money. She had not known this kind of friendship since she lost Mary Claire to an order of cloistered nuns. Adelia and Ellie spent long hours together walking the beach, shopping, lunching, taking in plays, art exhibits and parties. And talking, the women were always talking and laughing. Now on a rainy Tuesday morning Adelia and Ellie sat at their favorite coffee place at a chrome kitchen table with a green Formica top. Mary Claire's family had a chrome kitchen table with a green Formica top. Adelia had felt secure sitting with Mary Claire's family around that table. She felt the same security sitting at this table with Ellie. There was a comfort in things from her school days. Formica topped tables, sectional davenports, black and white television sets with little screens and thick backs, chunky lamps, cars with fins and soda fountains that served cherry sodas, and letter sweaters all made her feel warm and safe. Something she thought about as she ate one of the huge cinnamon rolls for which Broadway Brew was famous. The roll was so fresh the smell of its baking still lingered in the air.

Ellie on her second bagel spread with vegetable cream cheese talked about the need to watch her weight while she watched the customers. They came in groups of twos or three and greeted those gathered before they ordered coffee to take to a table or one of the stuffed chairs in the game corner. Ellie started at a girl who looked barely sixteen and brought in her painting, an oil abstract; and watched Katie hang it with the other work of young artists that covered the coffee house walls. Adelia felt comfort in being one of a group of caring people connected by an undefined thread of friendship. Slowly she was beginning to understand her son's reason for wanting to be a part of this society. Yet the comfort she felt frightened her.

A young man entered the shop and asked about buying one of the few books left from a local author's signing party the day before stacked near the cash register. Kate's sister-in-law a petite nineteen year old with bouncy hair and a contagious smile working behind the counter sold him one and he sat with it at a red Formica topped table. "Lot about your family in this book, Ellie," he said.

"Oh," Ellie responded her voice so cold Adelia hardly recognized it.

The boy left and Adelia asked about him.

"He is one you can't trust. He'll suck up to you for your money," Ellie whispered before she went back to eating.

Adelia surprised by Ellie's attitude toward the boy sought to change the subject when Ellie looked out at the Central Emporium just across Broadway Street and started to reminisce about the summers long ago of the auctions when the deserted dance hall filled with treasures opened after being closed for many years and a marathon of auction sales began. "So much history so many antiques dissipated to the auctioneer's call," Ellie commented.

Adelia treasured a stemmed antique glass etched with a sun and the word *Mission* for Mission orange drink. She once lovingly packed two and cried on the rainy day Charlie then three threw one down and it shattered. Charlie couldn't have known how precious the glasses were

to her. She never told him of the hot day and the crowd at the auction. He never knew about her seeing the two glasses, a pair, sitting
on a corner of the table and wanting them or his biding a weeks salary
against a lady from an antique shop. Or that night opening a can of beer
with a punch opener they called a church key. To Adelia the memory of
him slowly pouring beer in the two glasses and making a toast "to us,
together forever" was still vivid. When the glass broke it was a painful
reminder to Adelia she would never know her dream.

Then Adelia realized Ellie was talking about something else. She
was trying to coax Adelia to play bridge at the Yacht Club Bridge party.
Adelia said she hardly played. She had taken bridge lessons at Joe's
instance and joined two Bridge clubs. The ladies in one of her bridge
clubs were older than she and when several members died they were
not replaced and the club ceased to exist. The second club had so many
members move away those left just quit meeting. Adelia had not played
a hand of bridge in a decade.

Ellie had been insistent. Now Adelia sat with a good hand not certain how to bid it with her partner glaring at her indecision. Only after
Adelia bid and made a small slam in spades did the woman even smile
satisfied by the 180 plus 500 for a small slam on her scorecard. After
that Adelia started to have a reasonable time until she met her last partner a woman about her own age identified as Sally.

Sally more engrossed with her position as chairperson of the Yacht
Club August social than her bridge game ignored Adelia when she
moved up to her table and asked who had drawn low. Sally was talking about the caterers being reluctant to do egg rolls and didn't answer
Adelia's request. Finally the woman Sally was talking to directed Adelia
to the chair across from Sally.

Neither Adelia nor Sally could bid the first hand. They helplessly defended
a six no trump bid that made seven tricks. Sally opened the second hand with
two clubs, Adelia was unsure whether Sally was employing a convention
or had the necessary point for a two opener but with six small clubs and an
ace of spades and an ace of hearts jumped to five. Sally frowned until Adelia
laid her hand down. It was a fit at the five clubs and Sally handily made the
bid but still had not spoken directly to Adelia. Adelia complimented Sally on
playing the hand Sally barely acknowledged the compliment. The bid on the

next four hands went to the opponents. Sally played bridge poorly and the opponents' bids were made in two hands she and Sally should have set.

Sally left the table momentarily. One of the other woman at the table commented, "Hope you were not offended by Sally. She treats everyone that way. I don't know how her husband puts up with it."

"Thank goodness he has his dog," the other woman interjected. "He has always loved those big yellow dogs."

Adelia said nothing. Sally must be Agnes' daughter-in-law. If she were, Agnes had every right to dislike her.

Adelia wanted to quiz Ellie about Sally on the drive back to the east side of the lake but thought better of it. Ellie was not talking. She got low prize. It hurt her ego. Only when she was getting out of the car did she comment, "Dam that Sally Luc when she was my partner she had three good hands and she blew them all."

"Sally is not a favorite partner," Adelia carefully ventured.

"The lady is an egotistical idiot. It is bad enough to be dumb or egotistical, but to be both is too much. She causes my blood to boil. Poor Max she trapped him. He is too kind to dump her. He had an affair a few years back with Sissy, one of Sally's nieces. I don't know what happened. The niece is married now although not happily to a boy close to her age. Some say Max broke it off. Sissy can spend money as fast as Sally." Ellie got out of the car then without saying anymore. Adelia was so preoccupied she drove four blocks past Tennessee before she realized where she was.

CHAPTER XV

Eighteen days Joe lay in St. Matthew Hospital Adelia trying to will him well. She rarely left his side afraid if she did, he would slip away in her absence. On the nineteenth day at six o'clock in the morning Charlie whispered to her. "Mom, go for a walk. The cool morning air will be good for you."

Two hours later she returned. Joe's eyes were closed. He died at four o'clock the next morning, never having woken.

She and Charlie left his body in the cold hospital room and through his tears Charlie said, "Dad's last words to me were that he loved me more than he could have loved a son. Why would he have said that mom?"

"Because he loved you more than you knew Charlie. You gave him so much."

Charlie said nothing more but looked at his mother in a strange way. Adelia's heart was lighter. She had not answered Charlie's question. He did not ask again. The burden she carried for nearly three decades was no longer with her.

The month after Joe died Adelia followed Charlie to Charlottesville. She couldn't stay at the Boarshead; the memories of being there with Joe were too vivid. She took a room and breakfast with Mrs. Martha Sue McGroder in a two-story colonial on Barracks Road. Mrs. McGroder rented for companionship not money. Adelia was glad for her company. Charlie busy editing the law review, studying for classes and bar exams had little time for his mother.

61

Mornings Adelia lingered over breakfast with Mr. McGroder and then emerged herself in the history of the region seeking to find from the lives of those before a reason for her to continue to live. She spent two days walking the University grounds. She drove to Williamsburg and stayed two nights at the Williamsburg Inn roaming the streets of the colonial city.

On a sunny day she drove south to Virginia Beach and took the bay tunnel bridge to the eastern shore. There she sat for hours on deserted beaches and found an old inn where alone at a table she ate fresh from the sea soft shell crab sautéed in butter. Driving back to Charlottesville she stopped at York and toured the grounds where many men lost their lives. She dwelled on the bravery of the women whose sons, husbands, brothers were killed in battles. Monuments of battles were everywhere. Celebrating and honoring violence had always been a part of life. The colonial women who toiled to provide life's simple necessities for their families had no monuments built for them.

Back in Charlottesville on a clear afternoon Adelia visited The Colonnades, the senior living community, on 59 acres in the foothills of the Blue Ridge Mountains located close to the University of Virginia. The residents were active older people took advantage of the opportunity to participate in classes and cultural events at the University. There was no more perfect place for Adelia to spend her golden years, particularly with Charlie intending to take a job near Charlottesville.

It rained and thundered early on the day she and Martha Sue drove to Appomattox Courthouse. Finally the sun again appeared making the day hot and muggy. Adelia and Martha Sue sat in the grass at the spot where the civil war started and ended and tried to hear the troops marching, some in victory and others in defeat. They talked of the soldiers from the north and the south who fought not for their own freedom but for the freedom or slavery of others. Adelia asked if the young boys drawn to the battlefield had understood the reason for the confrontations. Did they know why their country was divided? And what of their mothers, wives and sisters many who did not believe in the battle yet were left without their men or saw them return disabled, worn and old beyond their years.

On the drive back to Charlottesville Adelia and Martha Sue talked that their families fought the war on different sides. Martha Sue remembered the hatred her grandfather carried for the northerners.

Charlie joined Adelia that night at the Virginian for a quick meal. She hugged him when he rose to return to the library and sought to find solace in that he did not have to go to war. She scolded herself for her depression. Her crosses were lighter then those of women before her.

Two days later in the early morning Adelia went to Charlie's room on the lawn. He sat in a rocking chair near his door wearing a dark green terry bathrobe, his hair wet and his face unshaven. Interrupting his solitude she asked if he sat thinking of the men who had lived on the Lawn before him in rooms where the paint now peeled and the door didn't want to close and the floors lay uneven and scuffed from generations of feet. He smiled. Adelia told her son she felt it would be wrong for him to marry Jane. "It is wrong," she nearly shouted. He listened rocking gently and looking to the Lawn not to her. She finally finished unable to share her true fear. Still rocking he took her hand and patted it. His only words, "I love you, mother."

She turned and walked away knowing for the first time in all her years with her son nothing she said or did would change his mind. Their relationship would forever be changed. She returned two days later to Chicago possessed with the nagging fear her darkest secret was no longer safe. Charlie called his mother two weeks before graduation to tell her he and Jane would be married the next August. She did not go for graduation. She had dreamed about seeing her son march on the lawn, receive his diploma, follow the path of Jefferson. Jane's parents would watch not she. Afterwards Charlie and Jane would drive back to Iowa with them. It was almost more than Adelia could bear.

Yet she was ill prepared for Charlie's call the next month to tell her he and Jane had taken jobs in Iowa. Adelia grieved. She planned Charlie would stay near Charlottesville. She was making arrangements for an apartment in the Columns. She would never visit Charlie in Iowa. He could never know why.

CHAPTER XVI

Once revealed secrets
are no longer secrets
and when secrets
are revealed they
open doors to other
secrets

ADELIA HOGAN

On a Sunday in late June Ellie took Adelia to eight o'clock Sunday Mass at St. Joseph's Catholic Church in Milford where Jane and Charlie would exchange vows. After Mass the women sat drinking big cups of good breakfast blend coffee and sharing a bagel with jalapeno and raspberry crème cheese on the porch at the Broadway Brew. Adelia read the Des Moines Sunday Register until Ellie interrupted her, "How did you meet him?"

"Him?" Adelia asked cautiously.

"Your husband, Joe."

"Oh, Joe." Ellie looked at Adelia strangely.

But she continued, "I needed a job. I was orphaned at nine. My grandmother finished raising me. She died before I finished high school. There was no money. I answered Joe's ad in the neighborhood shopper for a housekeeper. His wife of twenty-eight years, a heavy smoker, died some months before of lung cancer. The interview was to be at Charlie's

Diner. Joe was late. I sat in a front booth. I ordered a Pepsi with ice and when Joe came he ordered banana crème pie. He said Charlie made it fresh every morning. Nervous I declined the pie but only after he finished his pie did he start to talk."

"And?"

"He asked me if I could keep house. I said I thought I could and bared my soul about my need to find a job. I sensed he was a kind man but boring. He asked me if I would take the job if it were offered. I assured him I would. Joe told me he would check with my prior employer. If they gave me a good reference he would hire me. He asked me to call him the next afternoon at four. I did; he told me the job was mine."

"It was years later one Sunday Joe and I had taken Charlie to see New York City. Charlie was with friends. Joe and I were walking in Central Park and he told me he never checked my reference because if it were not good he would have hired me anyway."

"Your life was hard," Ellie said sympathetically.

"Until Joe hired me then it slowly stated getting easier. The next day Joe picked me up in his black Cadillac, a model that still had the big fins in back. I had never ridden in such a car. Yet I was not prepared for the size of his six-bedroom home. I had two boxes and a blue Samsonite train case that was my pride and joy. My grandmother got it for me with Green stamps just before she died."

"I remember Green stamps," Ellie interrupted. "My mother gave hers to the kitchen help."

"My grandmother saved every stamp. They were the only way we could buy special things."

"Our lives were different. I remember the luggage too. It was extremely heavy. In my group you had to have a matching set of five or six pieces before college. It was a statement you were going places. For two years for birthdays I got luggage. I left for college having six pieces including the train case and the hatbox. Mine were in matching green." Ellie finished her monologue and took another sip of coffee before she looked Adelia in the eye and said again in a surprised way, "Your life was hard."

"Until I moved in Joe's house. My bedroom at Joe's, the maid's quarters he called it, was behind the kitchen, such splendor, two big rooms, one a bedroom, one a sitting room and a bathroom with both a tub and shower and a bidet. I didn't know what the bidet was and Joe's face turned red when I asked him. He never did answer that question. Oh and I also had my own television. I turned it on and saw the NBC Peacock in color for the very first time. The best thing of all was my own pink PRINCESS telephone with a light up dial but I had no one to call."

A boy and girl who looked not to yet be twenty ran hand and hand from a car into a shop across the street. Adelia's eyes followed them.

"Did you ever have a young lover?" Ellie queried.

Adelia chose not to answer but continued her story telling Ellie two months after she went to work for Joe they were married at lake Tahoe in a commercial wedding chapel. "The guy who married us told me I would be sorry for marrying such an old coot and assured Joe I only wanted his money."

"Doesn't sound like a happy wedding day?"

"Joe adored me." Inside Adelia lay the memory of her fright before Joe. The wedding gave her a family and money. That there was no love she accepted.

"But did you adore him?" Ellie pried.

Pretending not to hear the question Adelia continued, "We spent the night at his house on Lake Tahoe and the next day flew from Reno to Mexico City. I threw up every morning and didn't quit until mid-afternoon."

"The food in Mexico can do that to you."

"It wasn't the food. I was pregnant." She stopped startled by her revelation.

Ellie sensed her shame. "I was pregnant when I married Windsor," Ellie blurted out. "But I was worse than you. It wasn't with his child. I had an affair with a guy six feet five with curly brown hair who went to Michigan. I really thought he loved me. I called him on Valentine's day to tell him, he was going to be a father. He told me he was not going to be a father and I should get money from my rich father and have an abortion. I left college and came up here to the family cottage. I looked up Windsor. I had several dates with him the prior summer. Three days later we went to Jackson, Minnesota to be married. I thought I convinced Windsor I got pregnant on our wedding night and Mickey was three months premature. Later when I was to accuse him of lying to me about his girl friend, he said two could play the game of deceit. But he surely enjoyed my family money."

Adelia put the comic section in front of her face not wanting Ellie to see the tears.

"No other guy will get to my money," Ellie added as an after thought. Then as if to change the subject Ellie said, "You have to watch an Okoboji Yacht Club race." When Adelia tried to regret the invitation Ellie told her, "You don't truly understand Okoboji until you have seen one."

A week later on a hot windy Sunday morning Ellie picked Adelia up in her red motorboat. Leaving Adelia's dock Ellie headed straight across the lake to where a large boat flying a number of flags sat anchored while boats with white sails all bearing the letter P sailed around it. "The boat flying the flags is the Yacht club judges boat," Ellie explained. In a few minutes we will hear the first in the sequences of guns alerting the sailors the race will be starting and they need to ready themselves."

Ellie had hardly finished talking when the sound of a gun frightened Adelia and she notice many in the boats pull stopwatches from around their necks and set the time. There was a ten-minute pre start sequence and then the boats started at five minutes intervals. Ellie explained that the first boats to cross the imaginary starting line between the judge boat and a buoy to its side were C Boats. They carried a large single sail. Ellie related that the seasoned adult sailors sailed those boats. After the C boats came M16 boats carrying a main sail and a jib, a small sail on the boat's front. The M16's were sailed generally by the college age sailors. The X Boats skippered and crewed by youngsters less than sixteen years of age started last. Ellie explained it took her years after her children completed their time as X sailors not to get up tight when the X boats started.

"I remember well the years they sailed. They started at eight. They were on the boats alone with a crew. I would coach them in my mind, but they couldn't hear me yell. It was a family sport. Brother and sister would sail against and sometimes with each other. Sometimes the younger ones would sail on the right side of the course or the older ones would get dead air. It was hard when the younger one won, but that was life. Age, position nothing really assured you success if the wind does not fill your sail. And Ellie continued, our entire family was out here together as were other families. Those children grow up closer than most children are to their siblings. Sailing was a family thing and because it was done as a family the older children accepted the younger children as equals. I believe that is one of the reasons the kids love to come back. I think that is why Jane came back. Charlie is accepted because he is marrying Jane."

Adelia knew she was right. She felt the closeness. A shared love and understanding. People caring about others; people knowing others. Charlie was an only child and she and Joe had no friends with children his age. He had grown up alone. Now he was part of the Abbott family. The thought of it all increased her jealously of Jane yet in her heart was envy and a wish that she too could be part of this lake's family.

CHAPTER XVII

I put on my best cloths
my best manners
to enjoy the party
sometime in the festivities
my life seemed to have stood still.

Adelia Hogan

Charlie only told his mother he was taking her to a cocktail party. Adelia chose a shirtwaist deep apostle flowers on a beige background. The wide matching belt nipped her slender waist. She was admiring herself in the full-length mirror in the bathroom when Charlie sounded the horn at six. Jane sat in the back seat and Adelia slide in the front next to her son. "Where is this party?"

"At Kettleson's. Jane calls it a show off party," Charlie remarked

"Oh," Adelia started to interject.

As Jane continued "Arnold Kettleson is an orthodontist. Daphne Kettleson is an orthodontist's wife. Theirs is just one of the new houses on the lake built by summer residents trying to out do each other."

"Kettleson." Adelia had not realized she said the name out loud. She should tell Charlie she had suddenly taken sickly and wanted to go home when Jane continued.

"Yes, Kettleson, I'm catty Adelia, but I've seen many parents sacrifice to have him put braces put on their child's teeth. The Dental school controls the number of orthodontists they let out to practice. Orthodontists charge plenty. They make more money than they know how to spend. Yet the assistants in their offices hardly make a living. It is that way in the entire medical profession. The schools limit the ones that get doctor degrees. I admire those who do. Yet the others, the nurses and technicians and aids, the ones who hold the patient's hand, they are knowledgeable but have no degree. They make little."

Adelia found herself smiling. Jane showed a compassion Adelia had not seen before and for that brief moment Adelia almost liked her.

"Money," Jane continued an edge to her voice, "it is all about money."

The words frightened Adelia. Neither Charlie nor Jane know how wealthy she was or how her fortune accumulated and was accumulating. They did not know Joe made his money from a patent for an artificial hip. Joe never wanted anyone to know. Adelia only learned after his death. Jane didn't know Adelia like the doctors made more money than she knew what to do with coming from her patent rights in a medical device. Really Charlie was no different. His law degree gave him a key to the legal gates. Adelia remembered Joe's complaints about lawyers over charging. Before Adelia said anything they pulled in the Kettleson drive way behind Ellie in a new red convertible. Anxious to talk to Ellie Adelia decided she would go to the party.

The three story Kettleson house over powering the fifty-foot lake shore lot on which it was constructed still had stickers on the third floor windows and roll lines on the sod in the yard. Adelia and Jane waited for Charlie to park the car as Ellie joined them.

"Glad you are here Adelia. I almost thought better of coming. Arnold's first wife Betty was a good friend. They divorced seven years ago and Arnold married Daphnie Duffey. Daphnie is younger then Arnold's kids and she wanted a baby. Poor Arnold had to have his vasectomy reversed to make it happen. Now he has two babies younger than his youngest grandchild."

"Ellie you always have the scoop," Jane chided her.

"What is more Jane it is Dickie's Deli again tonight." Ellie looked to the white truck with red letters parked in the driveway. "Broccoli, cucumbers, baby carrots, celery, wafer thin tasteless pressed turkey, ham on cocktail buns, potato chips, sour cream and onion dip and mustard and pickles."

"And big bowls of mixed nuts with lots of peanuts," Charlie interjected coming closer.

"The menu of the new rich, money but no class. Betty had class. And could she cook. No baby carrots and dip on her table." Ellie didn't smile. " I suppose Arnold finds sex better with Daphnie. Wonder if he is truer to her than he was to Betty?"

Adelia cringed.

A two-story foyer led to a living room where one wall of windows framed the lake. To the right was a dinning room where several women in white uniforms were putting plastic trays covered with high plastic domes on the table. To the left a library, shelves but few books. Adelia wandered. The interior designer had done her thing and no one touched anything since. Each item correctly chosen looked sterile in its perfection. Two ladies in a corner talked about the orthodontists, their big houses and that straightening teeth had to be the most lucrative profession.

"Be hell to stand by a chair all day looking at acne-covered faces and tightening wire on teeth," the other interjected. They deserve what they have."

"You can buy houses and furniture. You can't buy education and culture," the first woman continued.

Adelia retreated. Had Joe's educated friends said those things about her? She had not even graduated from high school. Her grandmother's death prevented it. Was that why Joe encouraged her books, travels, bridge and writing classes at the university. Always when his friends talked of their college days, she felt left out. She wanted to go to college. Sister Kathleen her high school English teacher said she should and that she could get a scholarship. It did not happen. Even today she envied anyone who went to college. She told Charlie he was going to college from the minute he was born. She wanted him to be more than she was. She never thought sending him to college in Virginia he would meet a girl from Iowa.

A man came up. The hair on his head was not his. He extended his hand. "I'm Dr. Kettleson," he said putting the accent on the word Doctor.

"Adelia Hogan, Charlie Hogan's mother, thank you for including me in the invitation." She looked the man over carefully and attempted to look straight in his eyes but they shifted. She sensed his discomfort and smiled. Seeing him again after all those years the nagging doubt she had carried that he could be Charlie's father was erased. She was right in concluding years ago that Charlie resembled her one true love. At least she wanted to hope that was true.

"The bar is on the front porch." Dr. Kettleson said quickly and walked on.

Adelia found a crowd near the bar. A young boy awkwardly worked filling the guests' orders. Adelia stood alone for a time before one of the women she had heard talking about the orthodontists came up. "You have to be Charlie's mother."

Nodding Adelia wondered if there were any secrets in this place. The familiarity caused her discomfort. She treasured her privacy. It was again interrupted by a brassy woman with a southern accent. "Welcome to Okoboji," the women said with out introducing herself.

"Thank you," Adelia tried to be polite.

"Dr. Kettleson asked me about you," the woman continued. Thinks he would like to get acquainted. Daphne is boring him. I think he craves the championship of a woman closer his age."

Adelia could only look at the woman after she insulted Adelia telling her he thought Adelia was as old as Dr. Kettleson and wondering if this total stranger was concerned about her or intent on destroying any respect she might have had for Dr. Kettleson. Thankful to see Charlie approaching Adelia moved towards him. The woman gave Charlie a flirty smile and moved on.

Charlie had brought his mother a glass of wine. The first sip told her it was cheap, came in a box or a bottle with a screw off top. Joe had taught her about fine wine. The kind you drank slowly, savored. Joe had education and culture. He had money. Why had she always yearned for more? Several guests told Adelia how handsome Charlie was, a fact she knew. Some said Jane and Charlie made a beautiful couple, a fact that raised her jealousy. One man said he trusted she enjoyed the area. He said it was so much better than Chicago with all its traffic. She was ready to argue a bit with him but was stopped by a man's laugh. Sure it was Charlie she turned. She did not see Charlie. A tall thin man behind her stood facing Sally Luc. Adelia stared at his back. His posture straight an expensive summer suit hung loosely on his body. Sally saw Adelia and turned toward her. "My bridge partner. Max meet this woman. We played bridge last week." Sally was off.

Max held out his hand. He tried to meet Adelia's eyes. She stared at her shoes. He spoke, "She doesn't remember your name, but I do."

Her memory of what he looked like had never dimmed but always he was young. His eyes slate blue were still friendly and sincere but sad. His hair was thinning and there were lines by his eyes and the corner of his mouth. The years could not be erased. Any question that he was not Charlie's father was erased. At least that was what she wanted to think.

"Bug," he squeezed her hand. He started gently stroking her palm. Afraid she quickly pulled her hand away.

"As beautiful and independent as ever." He looked at the wine glass in her hand. "See you have switched from Millers."

Her first taste of beer had come from a tall bottle of cold Millers with a gold band at the top. A wedding band he called it as he put in on her finger and she felt loved.

"I have dreamed about you every night for the last thirty years."

"My name is Mrs. Joe Hogan, sir. I don't know what you are taking about. Excuse me I have friends here." She had started to turn away when he gently grabbed her arm.

"I have not forgotten you. I have been looking for you since mother showed me the bracelet she said a friend gave her. Didn't you remember the night in the boat I gave it to you? You promised you would always wear it."

She detected a touch of hurt in his voice. She had kept her promise to wear it for nearly three decades yet she could say nothing. She could only walk away. He followed whispering, "Why didn't your answer my letters? Why did you disappear?"

Adelia's hair was a different color. The space between her teeth was gone. She was nearly thirty years older. He would think he was mistaken. That was not what she wanted but it was the way she had to make it. She had been foolish to befriend Agnes.

"Sir I have no idea what you are talking about. Unless you leave me alone I will tell our host you are harassing me."

"Wouldn't bother him. He has spent his life harassing women or have you forgotten?"

Thankfully Sally appeared and pulled Max away to introduce him to someone. Adelia started counting the days until the wedding. The day after she could leave.

Charlie and Jane dropped her off at Tennessee. She fell in bed and cried herself to sleep. The birds were well into their morning chorus before she woke from a fitful sleep. The sun shone brightly and the lake sparkled but her mood did not. She wanted to run but did not know where to go.

CHAPTER XVIII

on a soft morning
fresh flowers
sent with a greeting
'I love you'

fresh flowers
sent without a greeting
what message do
they bring?

Adelia Hogan

At ten o'clock the telephone rang. Would Adelia Hogan be home? The Flower Basket had a delivery. At ten thirty a young woman with a pleasant face delivered a bouquet. There was no card with the daisies, in pinks, yellows, and pale blues. The flowers gave a festive feeling to the room. Adelia put them on the mantel and stared at the stems in the clear glass vase. A bouquet of daisies once beautiful and now ugly and brown, were pressed in her memory book with a picture of a girl and a boy taken in a photo booth. Those daisies had been a gesture of love. They had come on a hot summer morning. The night before there had been ugly words. The card with those daisies said, "I'm sorry, I love you." The card too was in her memory book where she had looked at it often.

Adelia called the Flower Basket to see who sent the flowers. The man who answered said he did not know. Adelia did not believe him. Maybe Charlie sent them. Adelia found herself hoping he did not.

CHAPTER XIX

mysteries,
memories,
guilt,
hope,
dreams

Ellie called fifteen minutes before noon. A poet with some local fame was scheduled to give a two-day seminar on poetry at the Lakes Art center. They needed two more people to assure that he would come. Ellie was going would Adelia. Adelia impressed with the educational and cultural events the area offered said no. Ellie seemed to sense her mood. "You sound depressed. Lets meet at Broadway Brew for coffee."

"No. I must go." Adelia hung up the phone with no explanation. She wanted only to be alone to read, walk the lakeshore and sort out her conflicting emotions. She walked for miles not knowing where she was going or where she had been. At nine o'clock she sat on the bank of the lake studying the sunset of pinks and blues and golds and tried to write a poem capturing the beauty and failed. It was as if she had been drained of all feeling and emotion.

The next day she spent a short hour with Agnes who seemed restless and distracted. Agnes told her one did not appreciate what it was to be young until you are old and then closed her eyes. Adelia needed to talk to Agnes. She needed her to listen. The older woman started to snore. Adelia kissed her forehead. Agnes smiled in her sleep and Adelia left the room. An aid in a stained uniform frowned at her in the hall. The employees at Lakeview appeared over worked and unhappy. Adelia wondered how to help.

Adelia stopped at the garden store. She bought two flats of red geraniums marked half price and a big bag of potting soil. There were two big clay pots in the storage room at Tennessee. She filled them with loose moist soil and tenderly planted the flowers. The soft dirt felt good between her fingers and provided some solace. For a few brief moments her mind wandered to the times she and Joe worked in the garden, surrounding their home. The memories brought tears.

Inside she made red clam chowder with fresh garlic, parsley, tomatoes, basil and oregano and canine pepper and canned minced clams. The aroma of it cooking should have made her hungry but it did not. She ate a cracker and cooled the chowder and placed it in a covered dish in the refrigerator.

Charlie called as blackness fell. He told his mother he would pick her up in forty-five minutes. She resisted. He said he would be there. She should dress casually. He was taking her dancing. Adelia tried to tell him she didn't dance but he had hung up.

She chose a pair of light blue walking shorts and a blue silk blouse. Charlie was there as promised explaining he was taking her to Murphy's to hear a local band.

She asked where Murphy's was and he laughed. "Two doors from your coffee shop mother or don't you notice bars?"

"Oh."

"Don't be a prude mother. The vocalist and saxophone player in the band are clients. They were injured in a car accident. It is a good case. Clients like that ask you to come to hear them perform, you do. Jane works tonight. You are my next best girl."

Being alone with her only child raised Adelia's spirits. They arrived at Murphy on Broadway Street at twenty-eight minutes past nine. Customers were just beginning to gather at the Night Club. Adelia asked for a beer. The bar tender offered a full range of domestic and imported beers and the house specialty MURPHY'S MAD ALE. Adelia ordered the MAD ALE and Charlie followed suit. Adelia had finish nearly half her pint of the dark mellow beer when a tall muscular good-looking man about thirty thin and with a pleasant smile approached their table.

"Bar tender says you're a new lawyer. Grew up with Jane. She is a neat woman. I'm Murphy." He shook Charlie's hand.

"Murphy this is my mother Adelia Hogan. I've heard about you. Some friends of mine at Tahoe said your name when they learned I was moving to this area. Seems you have a reputation as a skier."

"Like it. Do you ever water ski Charlie?"

"Not much but I enjoy it."

Adelia smiled remembering her son's feeble attempts at staying up right.

"We'll take you out some afternoon. The Boartworks just set me up with a new boat."

"Thanks."

"See you are drinking my ale," Murphy commented.

"Great ale," Charlie said and Adelia nodded her assent.

Murphy left. Charlie smiled at his mother. "They say that guy is the best water skier around. I think I'll be busy when he calls to water ski. I don't want to make a fool of myself."

Sipping the ale Adelia studied the fascinating collection of lake memorabilia, antique bicycles, ice skates, musical instruments, snow skis, signs and lake trash that covered the walls of the club.

The band loud started to play. A young man challenged Charlie to a game of pool. He hesitated. His mother insisted he play. A couple in their early twenties still dressed in swimming suits swayed on the dance floor. Adelia turned her beer glass in her hand unaware someone stood watching her.

He walked towards her table, stood over her and spoke. "No Bing cherries for sale today."

Adelia recognized the voice but did not look up. She tried to look puzzled and stared at the table afraid to look in the speaker's eyes. He ignored her gestures of unfriendliness and continued. "I close my eyes and see you standing barefoot over by the bar, lots of leg showing, picking cherries from a crate one by one."

"Sir, leave me alone. I don't know what you are talking about." Adelia wanted to call for Charlie but did not, afraid he would ask questions.

"This used to be the grocery store or have you forgotten?"

"Please go." Her voice was weak. She had wanted it to sound like a command.

"I'll have this dance and you can tell me why I don't know you."

He took her hand. She found herself following him to the dance floor. Stepping to the beat, he held her close. He used the same shaving lotion. She had not forgotten the smell. The twenty year olds looked at them strangely and laughed to themselves. The music loud he talked directly in her ear. "I wrote you letters. I came to Chicago that winter. Bought a bus ticket just to see you. The telephone number you gave me was disconnected. I looked in every face in the city trying to find yours. I waited for you the next summer. Cried when Karla told me, you called midwinter to tell her to hire someone else. I wrote to your address for years. I would call information in every city hoping to find you had a number listed there so I could talk to you. You broke my heart and ruined my life. Why?"

"My grandmother died after I returned home." She realized her mistake before she finished the sentence. But she had to continue; "I didn't see your letters for more than a decade."

"So Bug, ready to drop the charade."

"Don't tell anyone you knew me before or that I spent my seventeenth summer as Karla's summer girl."

"Oh."

"Charlie can't know."

"What prize is there for my silence?" He looked at her in a strange way.

"Please as a favor," she added weakly.

"Why do I owe you a favor when you broke my heart?"

"I didn't break your heart. You broke mine. I loved you. But you found another girl even before I was gone."

"No only you."

"I should be flattered, but I don't believe you."

"I meant it when I said I thought about you every night, three decades' worth."

Adeila was living her daily dream and worst nightmare. Max held her closer. She felt an excitement. She thought of what Ellie said about coming back here summers and sometimes for a brief moment capturing the magic of youth. She wanted to tell him about all the time he crept into her thoughts and how after finding his letters she wanted to make contact with him but she couldn't and wouldn't, not now, not ever.

The band took a break and Max led her to a table as Charlie approached. "Promised to have you home early mom." He took her arm. She smiled at Max as her son guided her into the night.

"See you met Max," Charlie commented as he helped her in the passenger seat before closing the door. "He is a great guy. "Funny I sat at his table at Rotary last week and a guy at our table said we looked alike."

Her son's words brought joy to her heart.

The car door closed and she failed to hear the rest of his comment. "Too bad he needs to file bankruptcy. He just keeps looking for any way out of doing it."

CHAPTER XX

Years evaporate
youth cannot be recaptured
what are the risks
in unearthing old passion?

ADELIA HOGAN

Charlie quickly dropped his mother off. Adelia sat on the cool grass near the lakeshore. Now and then the spark of a firefly broke the darkness. The moon, a crescent was slung low in the heavens dotted with stars there for viewing. An occasional breeze teased the oak trees and the waves tapped a gentle rhythm on the shore. It was a night for dreams. A night a married man and a widow shared a special moment. To him a recaptured memory; to her the revival of passions she sought for years to repress. Finally she went inside and soaked in water sweetened with bath oil in the ancient claw footed bathtub. She slipped into a thirsty white terry cloth robe before she heard a noise at the back door.

Max stood on Adelia's back door step. "Hello Chip," she said quietly.
"I lost that nick name when I grew up."
"Have we grown up?"
He looked at her and smiled not prepared to answer. Max standing on Adelia's back step brought out her venerability. Finally he spoke, "Wanted to be certain you were tucked in."
"Thank you." She moved to shut the door.

"You must believe I went to Chicago that winter. Called the number you gave me. When the operator said, it was out of service I argued with her. I looked at every face in Chicago knowing I would see yours."

"You have told me this all before."

"I wasn't sure you heard me."

"I did."

"I meant it when I said I have thought about you every day and night."

Once she believed everything he said. She was older now, hopefully wiser. He had a wife. What was he doing at her door?

"May I come in?"

Adelia tightened the sash on the thick terry cloth robe covering her naked body. Her voice flat she said, "I don't think so."

"For a few minutes?" He did not wait for an answer but stepped across the sill. She not prepared to stop him when he took her arm and led her toward the living room shutting the door behind him. She smelled his after shave and tried to detach herself from the man who stood next to her.

"Didn't you ever tell Charlie about our summer?" he queried.

"No, and don't you." She prayed she sounded firm. "It was a short summer years ago. It is best forgotten."

"Maybe for you it was short. For me it is a memory etched in my mind. I never forgot it; I always hoped for this second chance."

Why was he talking of a second chance?

"Please tell me our time together was important to you." Max was begging.

"It was then," she said without emotion. He had bared his soul. She owed him that little bit. She had never forgotten him. He did not deserve to know that.

He carried a brown sack from which he removed a bottle of wine. He found a corkscrew and glasses in the kitchen and poured wine for each of them. The first glass went down quickly. It was good wine not the boxed variety at the Kettleson's party. Why had she gone to that party? Why had she come to this place? Having no answers Adelia sat uncomfortably on a corner of the living room couch while Max filled each of their wine glasses a second time.

"I like your son, Adelia. You have done a good job."

"Thank you."

"God I wanted kids. Sally did not. Said she was selfish and wanted time for herself. I thought after several years I had convinced her and she just couldn't get pregnant. I decided there was something wrong with me. But Dr. Jack told me a couple years ago when he had too many martinis on hunting trip he always prescribed birth control pills for her. Twelve years ago Sally had a hysterectomy. She could no longer have kids. She whines about not having children and is insanely jealous of the nice things our contemporaries' children are doing. What relationship we had has been over for a very long time. I blamed it on the hysterectomy but that might not have been fair."

Max was revealing the intimate details of his life to a woman he had not seen in three decades.

He kept on, "it is hell to get old and know that your genes will die with you. There is nobody to carry my life forward. All that sperm will rot with me in the grave or go down the drain when the undertaker drains my blood. Charlie and Jane will have children. You will be a grandmother. I'll never be a grandfather. I thought about divorcing Sally and finding a young woman and trying to have kids with her. I carried on with a twenty-year-old for a while. I was a year older than her father. She flattered my ego. There were too many years and too little in common. I would always have to worry about her finding some young virile guy. If she did, my pride would be mortally wounded. You wounded it once. It could not survive again."

"I have a headache. You must go." Adelia said it gently. She didn't want him angry with her. She couldn't talk about this with him. He rose. She had told him to leave but did not want him to go. She would be alone. So many fragments of thoughts spun in her head.

She felt his finger massaging her temples. "My famous headache cure." Adelia smelled the after-shave. The wine had mellowed her resistance and the feel of his hand pleasurable she did not resist when his body moved closer. Then he got up walked to the door. She knew he had to leave but so wanted him close. She wanted to call out asking him to stay. But all she could do was sit silently.

He shut off the light and returned to the couch beside her. She let him pull her face to his and kiss her lips. She tried not to respond. Long ago she could not resist him. She was grown up. She was strong. She would not let it happen. He continued gently pushing her body down on the couch. The smell of his after-shave, strong it revived passions and she felt powerless to stop him. His hands caressed her body and he carried her to the bed in the middle room. He undid the tie on the robe. Her body exposed in the moon light he removed his clothing and pressed his flesh to hers. Only a moan came from her lips. Her whole being craved his love.

Once she said, "don't." It was a weak plea not a command. Silently she said the act of contrition and asked God's forgiveness for her sin. It was over and they rested. He gently stroked her face. "Why did I not marry you? I wanted to you know."

"Did you?"

"God I did. I chose you for my wife the first day I saw you and watched you eat bing cherries on the pier. I bribed Billie you know to bring you to sailing lessons."

"Then why?"

"Why did I not marry you? I couldn't find you. I was young and stupid."

"No why were you with another girl my last night here."

"How did you know?"

"I saw you in the car. She sat on your lap."

"Oh God." She thought she heard a sob. "You were leaving. I thought somebody else would erase the horrible lonesome feeling. It didn't."

"Don't you need to go home?" She was angry with herself for letting this happen.

"Why?"

"Sally."

"Sally", he said in a flat voice, "Sally is not in our bed."

She didn't ask more questions. He might be too proud to supply further answers. He held her close. She was awake when at four he rose from her bed and dressed. "You are leaving?" she queried

"Your honor. This is a small place."

She sat alone on the front porch. The beauty of the rising sun reflected in the western sky. More shades of blue captivated in the lake and sky then she could describe. Her eyes riveted on the contrast in the lake where the light breeze created ripples. The simple beauty brought some calm to her tortured soul. She had never wanted last night to end. In all the years with Joe she never felt such passion. She crawled back in bed. The pillow still indented from his head she drew it to her face and inhaled the slight scent of his after-shave.

CHAPTER XXI

I don't know who I am
how I came here
what it should be
why I'm still in love

ADELIA HOGAN

Elizabeth continued to orchestrate Adelia's life. Ellie was hosting her annual summer Saturday night bash. Elizabeth telling Adelia she knew it was hard for her to go places without an escort arranged for Adelia what she called 'a little date' with Simon Bowers. "One of the few available men our age," she whispered.

Simon had had at least two wives. After thirty minutes with him Adelia was certain they had to have divorced him. Elizabeth and Andrew were in Simon's ten-year-old Buick that had the aroma of the countryside, rust spots, a dirty floor and torn seats when Simon picked Adelia up.

Simon said he was taking them all to this lake restaurant for supper before the rich lady's party. Adelia had hoped to go directly to Ellie's. The menu Ellie planned promised that no one needed supper before the party.

The lake restaurant was actually a bar with a porch of sorts on the lake. Panels of plastic spoiled the view. They ordered beers that were served warm in cans with no glasses and brats that came on thin cheap paper plates with a single packet of mustard. Simon ate his quickly dribbling mustard on the collar of his flowered shirt. Adelia sipped the beer and listened to those around who seemed oblivious to the beauty of the lake and talked only of how fast their boat would go and how much beer they were drinking. All the natural beauty around, did they not see it?

Ready to leave Adelia's food still untouched. Simon commented he hated to pay for food not eaten. He took the brat off her plate and quickly wolfed it down. Elizabeth smiled apologetically at Adelia and she tried to return a smile. It barely came.

Ellie's party had started at six. It was past seven before they arrived and went immediately to the sweeping front-screened porch that gave a view of the lights on the west side of the lake. Missy the two hundred pound bar tender from Sweeties was smiling over the cooler of ice and the row of fine liquors and wines. In the dining room the huge dinning table was dressed in crisp white linen and lined with jumbo shrimp, cheeses, breads, fresh and marinated vegetables, spreads, pastas and pork tenderloin with horseradish and fine mustards.

Ellie's summer home, one of the lakes' original huge frame summer mansions was impressive. Original paintings of known and unknown artists hung everywhere. Simon stood over the food table sampling with his fingers directly from the bowls and platters.

Simon finally stopped eating and was talking to a woman Ellie told Adelia was a recently widowed and would inherit a clothing business. Adelia, Elizabeth and Andrew stood on the porch when Max walked behind where they stood.

"Good evening Mrs. Hogan."

Hearing his voice made Adelia weak but finally she managed a respectable, "Good evening."

"How are you Elizabeth?"

Adelia noticed Elizabeth blushed before she walked away. Had Max and Elizabeth once been lovers? Was hers the summer romance with Max that Agnes remembered?

Max stood there directly in front of Adelia. Andrew at her side Adelia searched for a topic of conversation to keep Max close.

"What are the political leanings in Iowa?" Adelia queried wondering what possessed her to ask the question.

"Lots of Republicans." He had taken the cue. "Years ago Democrats were too liberal to win many votes. But we Iowans are a strange sort, generally keep a United States Senator for more than six years and have one from each party. It may hurt us in some areas but probably helps us in others."

"And," Adelia wanted him to continue, to stay close.

"And it is a beautiful evening and I could stand here all evening talking to you."

He looked around and smiled at Andrew before continuing. "I'm talking softly. No one will hear but you. What are you doing with Simon? If he finds you have money he will never leave you alone."

"I asked you about politics," she replied mindful people were looking their direction.

"Iowa has the first presidential caucuses in the nation so we get all the presidential candidates for months before. There are jokes about everyone having to kiss an Iowa pig. That seems to be our national image, pigs. It couldn't be further from the truth particularly now when most Iowans complain about the smell of raising hogs and go to court to try to stop it. Iowans are a well educated, independent breed."

Sally put her hand on Max's shoulder then. "Max."

He pretended not to hear Sally. "Hope that answers your question." He winked at Adelia ever so slightly.

"Get me another gin and tonic," Sally commanded before fluffing off.

Max went to the bar. Elizabeth said Simon was ready to leave. As Adelia walked out the door, she saw Max hand Sally her drink walk to the porch and stand alone looking to the lake the muscles in his shoulders tight.

Elizabeth, Andrew and Simon, who by this time had talked non-stop with the clothing store widow, drove to Arnolds Park. They ordered espresso at Broadway Brew. Adelia paid. Simon made no attempt to even reach for his billfold. Loud music came from Murphy's and a long line waited at the door. Adelia thought of when it was the Arnolds Park grocery. Many years had passed since then. Why did she think she could recapture the youth and the love she lost when she married Joe? Why did she think she could once again sample the magic of her youth? Could it happen? She heard Ellie's words saying sometimes it did.

CHAPTER XXII

Is your religion to love God and
your fellow men accepting the frailties of their
souls?
Or are you determined to sculpture others lives to
yours
and seek out their weaknesses that by your defini-
tions are sin?
Do you fail to understand and love?
Yet take God's name and your bible
as your sword claiming they are your
right while ignoring that to be right
It is necessary to be kind.
And what dwells in your mind
Is it love or condemnation?
In self-searching are you seeking to understand,
to love and to forgive
Least it be easier to condemn
Others than to condemn your self and
to look to the castration of another man as a way
to avoid confronting your own sins.

ADELIA HOGAN

A Lake in Dickinson County

Adelia woke at seven with a splitting headache. She stayed up hours after Elizabeth and Andrew took her home opening a bottle of wine, writing in the lined notebook beside her bed and sipping wine until the bottle was gone. At eight Elizabeth had called to say that she needed Adelia to help do place cards. Twenty minutes later Jane rang saying they had decided to pay to have the place cards done in calligraphy. Adelia had been short with both women and now she regretted it.

Then came the call from Ellie rambling about the party and reciting who came and who didn't and that the caterer brought pork tenderloin when she had ordered all beef. She related about how Sally Luc stayed for two hours after the party though Max had left. Adelia had almost succeeded in cutting her garble off when Ellie confronted Adelia with, "What is going on with you and Max?"

"Nothing, why?" Adelia answered too quickly.

"You seemed interested in him at the party. I saw the way you looked in his eyes."

"Did somebody say something?"

"Elizabeth seemed surprised you talked to him so long?"

"She said that." Adelia hoped her voice had not betrayed her secret.

"Not exactly. I told her that it was your way of getting even with Simon for carrying on with the clothing store widow."

"Simon is a bore. And the guy has no manners."

"I know. He is also looking for a third wife with money. That is typical of guys our age."

"Oh," Adelia interjected thinking of Joe's caveat and Max's remarks last night.

Before she could say more Ellie continued. "The reason they look at us and not the young ones is that they think of the comfort our money can bring. Elizabeth sees you and Simon as single beings needing companionship. She was proud she lined you up. It is a hard thing for married persons to understand. I saw you as being more interested in Max. I may have been the only person who noticed the thing between you and Max last night. Though Elizabeth commented you seemed to be intent in engaging him in conversation about politics no less. Really Adelia people don't ask for lectures on the political climate of Iowa at cocktail parties. I'm your friend. The next person who notices might not be."

"Ellie."

"Adelia I don't deserve an explanation but it may be that you need a warning. It doesn't take much to set tongues wagging here. Max is in serious financial straights. I would hate to think he was after your money. You should know I heard him asking Andrew if you had done well financially. Andrew said you had."

Adelia was still fretting about Ellie's call when Charlie rang at five telling her he was grilling hamburgers and Jane was joining him and he would like Adelia to also.

Adelia begged off Charlie's invitation claiming her head ached. She took out her notebook and tried to continue writing the poem she had started the night before. She was surprised to find herself writing Mrs. Chip Luc.

Finally she looked up Max's phone number and dialed it. Sally answered. Adelia quickly hung up ashamed for making the call.

CHAPTER XXIII

The sky darkened
the winds built
until the noise
drove everyone inside
to watch from windows
the driving rain,
the thunder, the lightening
the inland wind could
have been a hurricane except
in short minutes it stopped
and when the sun reappeared
the yards were scattered with
branches and leaves and debris
three oak trees once tall
now bent, trucks shattered
but the people and the homes
were intact
soon the electricity was restored
and the summer storm
was relegated to a minor
place in the history of the land.

ADELIA HOGAN

Adelia awakened at four by thunder sat upright when a bolt of lightening struck near the front porch. The storm brought memories of Charlottesville and the summer Charlie stayed to work at the University and she and Joe visited. There were always storms in Charlottesville, several a day and the dark clouds hung low and the humidity was unbearable. She understood then why southern dames sat on verandas and drank mint juleps. The air conditioner at the Boarshead was set low to take the humidity out. There was an extreme contrast in temperature when she stepped outside. The rain showers hot and quickly over just as quickly returned. Then she wanted so badly to live in Virginia she didn't complain about the weather. She found Iowa summers more pleasant.

Adelia fell back to sleep and awakened to few signs of rain. The lush green of the tall oaks and the continuous morning medley of the songbirds lifted her spirits. A slight haze on the lake created a blue wonderment. The sky and lake seemed as one, almost like the ocean was still and silent before her.

Elizabeth suggested Adelia attend a lecture at the art center but she begged off, to read and write letters she said. Yet it was nearly ten before she finally finished the pot of morning coffee and sat on the patio with the stack of paper back books she bought several days earlier at one of the many a garage sales held every week end. The first books she quickly discarded and began reading Irving Shaw's *Rich Man, Poor Man*. It was a tattered paperback but the story was riveting, based on assents and descents in life and how positions shift in adulthood. Ironic she thought.

She was surprised at eleven thirty to have the phone ring and hear Max's voice. "Company, plans?" He inquired.

She could lie but didn't. "A book I planned to read and letters."

"I'll be there." He had hung up before she could protest.

She checked her hair and put on fresh under things and a print wrap around skirt and a favorite blouse. Waiting for Max Ellie's statements about Max's financial problems and Joe's warnings echoed in her head. Forty-five minutes later he slipped in the back door.

"I didn't hear a car."

"It is parked at the Inn. I walked on the beach."

"So no one will see you. What deceit."

"Not deceit good judgment." His arms were around her fondling her breasts.

The phone rang. It was Elizabeth asking her for supper. Worrying about her being alone.

"Supper I would."

He shook his head "no."

"I need to get my tasks finished and I won't if I don't stay with them. Thank you for asking." Gently she returned the phone to the cradle.

They sat on the screened porch all afternoon witnessed only by the tall oaks and the peaceful lake and kissed, petted and held each other close. Occasionally a powerboat would rush up or down the lake and break the silence.

"You should be here in early spring. The duck and mud hens fill the water and the occasional boat causes them to scatter."

"Interesting."

"You'll see next spring."

"I have ten days left here then I'm never coming back."

"Stay."

"Why so we can carry on an affair secretly and I can miss my home and friends and be the mother of the boy who married Jane Abbott." She stopped. There were not friends at home to miss. He should not know that.

"So we can be together."

She wanted to ask how they could be together in this place of many eyes and if he wanted her money. The phone rang. Ellie calling to go on and on about the thunder storm and having to call a tree service to cut off some branches the wind had broken that were hanging from the trunks. Adelia must have been short with her because she stopped quickly. "Max is there isn't he?" And then she hung up leaving Adelia puzzled. Max left at eight after telling her again and again he loved her. Adelia wanted to believe him. She wanted to ask if he would profess his love if she were poor. She offered to drive him to his car but he said no and walked out the back door. He was gone several minutes before she saw his jacket still hanging on a dining room chair. She put it on the smell of his after-shave sweet comfort as she read into the night.

C H A P T E R   X X I V

The appalling thing about war is that it kills all love of truth. Georg
Brandes. Letter to Geroges Clemenceau, March 1915

Robert McNamara
at age seventy-eight years
over thirty years ago
Secretary of the Department
of Defense under Lyndon Johnson
confesses
"the war in Vietnam should
not have been accelerated."
Why did McNamara wait
until his eight decade of life
to reveal the commands made
from the security of the oval office
to the young and strong
to destroy themselves and others
should not have been given?
What of 59.000 American soldiers,
who in life blindly
obedient to McNamara's call
were murdered on jungle floors?
their decayed bodies lay in graves marked
with flags by Legionaries
prayed over by their grieving parents

decorated by their children
who know them only
as names on tombstones.
McNamara's veracity today
Cannot correct the injustice.
It does resurrect the pain?

ADELIA HOGAN

August twenty-seventh started hot following an exceptional Iowa night when the temperature stayed near ninety degrees. A quarter inch of rain at nine in the morning settled the dust a bit. It watered the corn and beans, raised the farmers' spirits and left wispy dark clouds hanging low on the horizon and humidity collecting in the air.

At eleven Ellie arrived in her red boat to take Adelia across the lake to the brunch for Jane and Charlie at Marilyn and Rick Stockman's. Marilyn and Rick lived in a yellow continuum with white trim amidst twenty-five other yellow condominiums with white trim, similar floor plans and beige walls and almond middle of the line refrigerators with ice makers, stoves with self cleaning ovens and big tubs in the master suites. The condominiums fronted on the Harbors a series of channels dug thirty years earlier. Ellie said the canals should never been allowed to opened up to the lake. "Man should leave the terrain as nature created it. There has been too much building and moving of dirt around this lake. There will be a disaster," she pronounced.

Rick served a concoction he finally confessed was champagne, vodka and orange and pineapple juice from a flowered waste basket turn punch bowl on the front deck over looking the canal. Marilyn put out an egg, potato and cheese casserole, chunks of honeydew melon and cantaloupe and weak coffee on a table in the small dinning room of the beige upstairs.

Friendly people their hospitality contagious Adelia felt good until Simon cornered her. He apparently had not made it with the clothing widow. Ellie warned Adelia Simon learned Adelia had money that he did not know the night of Ellie's party. "If he had, he would have been more interested," Ellie said.

Adelia listened to Simon while her eyes scanned the room looking for Max. She had seen the guest list and knew he and Sally had been invited.

Charlie and Jane appeared both showing the strain of the wedding preparations. Andrew arrived saying Elizabeth was not feeling well and would not be coming. Adelia did not see Max before she and Ellie left in the red boat for a bar with a deck on the lake. There they sipped tall rums and cokes until nearly three when Adelia switched to iced tea. About that time Ellie began a conversation about her fear some guy would be after her for her money. The conversation disturbed Adelia. She quickly changed the subject.

CHAPTER XXV

Of the long ago
Secrets never shared
Jealousies of others
Happiness
Regrets for
Youth too quickly lost

ADELIA HOGAN

Adelia sensed someone have been in the cottage. The bolt was on the door. She couldn't quite place it but things seemed out of order. She called Charlie asking if he had been by and when he said no she started feeling uncomfortable. Then she saw Max's jacket was gone. How he had gotten in? That he had entered without her knowing raised her defenses.

Relieved to find her train case untouched in the bedroom she locked it with the key that hung around her neck and hid the case in the back of her closet. Adelia exchanged her heels for a pair of comfortable flat shoes before she locked the door and drove to the area of shops that Charlie called uptown Okoboji. She found a book for Agnes, candies, and a wool cover for chilly nights.

She drove then into the town of Arnolds Park and stopped at the Broadway Brew craving an espresso before heading home. Inside she found Max at the big yellow Formica table drinking coffee and sharing freshly baked oatmeal raisin cookies with a blond woman less than thirty.

Max greeted Adelia with a slow smile. She felt her face redden as she made a feeble attempt to respond to his greeting. He went back talking to the blond making no effort to introduce the women to each other.

Adelia planned to read the newspaper and drink her espresso at the shop. She should leave. There were other coffee shops. She had tried one once. The coffee tasted stale and no one smiled or made her feel welcome. She ordered her coffee to go. It served she quickly exited. Max in deep conversation with the young woman did not look up. Driving back to Haywards Bay her mind was full of Max and the young blond woman. She remembered what he said about dating a twenty-year-old and she tried to suppress jealously wondering how Max had gotten in her home and why he was so anxious to retrieve his jacket.

Jane was backing out of the driveway when Adelia arrived at Tennessee. Jane working on her wedding book wanted to gathered family trees and family comments. "Adelia would you write a couple of paragraphs for me on your feelings and Charlie's fathers comments when you knew Charlie was to be born." Adelia nodded slightly. Jane left then promising to call later.

The espresso had cooled. Adelia threw it out and poured a glass of cold ice tea from the glass jug in the refrigerator, squeezed a lemon wedge in the glass and took it to the front porch. She gazed at the gentle waves pushing into the bay trying to sort out her emotions. First there was Max's entry into her cottage and then his attention to the young woman at the table and now Jane's request. She couldn't write of her feelings of hopelessness those years ago when she learned after the funny little doctor at the Cook County Hospital stuck his fingers inside her that she was pregnant. Jane's wedding book would never carry the story of the times Charlie's mother laying in bed looking at her stomach willing to have an abortion and go to hell but having no money to pay for one. She couldn't write about Charlie's father's comments because she didn't know who his father was and he knew nothing about Charlie. He never knew Charlie was conceived.

Anger rose in her body. She uncertain if the anger were over the loss of her youth, jealously of the young or resentment that she never shared her secret.

CHAPTER XXVI

You came from me
though we are strangers
in and to ourselves
feeling only the pain
of our own bodies
able to shut out others pain
we want to love
yet our universe
is centered around our self
even among others
we are alone
the day our flesh rots
our bleak skeletons will stand
evidence of our solitude
but always we will be known
as mother and son

Adelia Hogan

At ten o'clock the thermometer still registered eighty degrees. Even the heaven full of stars seemed to radiate heat. At the grocery store the talk was no one could remember an August night this hot. The lake was peppered with boat lights their passengers looking for relief from the heat. The wedding was to happen day after tomorrow. Jane and her mother were surrounded with lists and relatives and friends.

Adelia feeling not wanted sat on the front porch of Tennessee drinking a too sweet wine cooler and looking up through the oak leaves to the stars trying to find the consolations. Occasionally she would hear a gentle rustle in the tress and a cooling wind would caress her body.

In the distance she heard either crickets or frogs, which she was not certain. Fireflies sparked nearby. She tried not to think of Max. She had not seen him since the day at the coffee house when his attention had been direct to the young girl. Tomorrow was the wedding rehearsal. Adelia hosting the groom's dinner had arranged for it at a guesthouse on the lake. The menu included fresh lobster flown in yesterday from Maine and fine champagne ordered specially by the local liquor store. The bride, groom, attendants, relatives and out of town people would be her guests. Sixty people and she the only relative Charlie would have present. She would suffer through the night the loneliness that came from of being a member of a crowd but not a part of it.

Adelia heard Agnes answer her phone. Adelia hesitated. She was uncertain why she had decided to call. Hearing Agnes's delight at being ask to be her guest at the rehearsal dinner she was glad she had. Hanging up she felt less lonesome.

CHAPTER XXVII

to once shinny wedding silver
the years bring tarnish
with soft cloth and the pasty polish
the wife lovingly rubs
until the shine reappears
but the pinta remains,
the elegance of aging,
lovingly caresses
reclaim the beauty
of an aging marriage
that like the silver
is more precious each year

Adelia Hogan

Elizabeth brought forth a silver punch bowl, coffee set, platters, and bowls. Her wedding gifts that were long hidden in cupboards were aging with tarnish and dust. Jane wanted them used for the reception. Adelia had joined Elizabeth and Jane on a sunny afternoon several weeks before the wedding to polish each piece until shinny. As the women rubbed on silver polish Elizabeth and Jane worried about supervising the florist in his decorating the morning of the wedding. Adelia finding happiness in being included in the festivities volunteered for the task.

Now on the day of her son's wedding she stood in the church the baskets of flowers, the rolled white runner, the nose gay bouquets marking the pews all in place. Seven o'clock Mass just concluded Father O'Donnell sat in the confessional on the north side of the church. Adelia looked at the little red light over the door showing Father was available to hear sins. Twice she nearly entered the confessional. The shame of the sins she must confess stopped her. Best she continued praying and confess her sins when she returned to Chicago to an unknown priest in a city church. Hers were not sins that should be confessed to the priest who in a few short hours would say a nuptial Mass and conduct a marriage. She would sit witness in the front pew on the right side of the church and the priests afterwards would sit next to her at the reception. Adelia would not bring that shame to her son. She prayed an act of contrition feeling dirty, unworthy and stained.

The flowers arranged Adelia drove to Broadway Brew hoping Ellie would have waken early enough to join her. She needed Ellie but found the coffee house empty except for a man who had laid claim to the morning paper and sat alone at the big yellow Formica table. She stayed though she didn't like to be seen alone. It was like she had nobody to be with. The cinnamon rolls still had not left the oven but filled the shop with their sweet aroma. Finally Adelia ordered and took her large cup of breakfast blend out to the porch. The day promised to be hot. A lone runner sweated profusely as she headed down Broadway Street towards the lake.

Adelia thought of calling Ellie but knew she enjoyed the opportunity to sleep in. Her friends were deserting her. Agnes called late afternoon yesterday she thought about Adelia's invitation. Rehearsal dinners were for friends and relatives of the bridal couple. She was neither. It wouldn't be right that she be there. She wouldn't attend. Adelia couldn't tell her she needed her there or that she should be there fearing if she had Agnes would question why she pushed.

The dinner was flawless, the food elegant and each guest sought out Adelia to express appreciation. Yet the whole evening Adelia felt hollow and detached.

She was seen as the widowed mother of the groom, the about to be come mother-in-law. Her matronly green dressed pressed hung in her closet. The shoes and purse dyed to match sat near by. She was losing her son. She had to hold her head up and try to smile. Tears flowed and she hardly realized Kate had put a hot roll on the table in front of her. She hoped Kate had not seen the tears. The smell of the roll tantalizing she ate it greedily and for a few moments its sweetness muted her pain.

CHAPTER XXVIII

The soft sweet music of a string quartet filled every crevice in the Gothic church. By four o'clock the three hundred or more guests had been ushered to their seats by Charlie's fraternity brothers handsome in rented black tuxes with green bow ties.

Jane stood on a sheet in the musty church basement. Adelia watched Elizabeth adjust her train for the fifth time. Andrew descended the stairs and looked fondly at his daughter. Adelia wished for the security of Joe's arm. Then Jim Thomas the head usher was at Adelia's side. He gently took her arm. "They are ready for the mother of the groom Adelia."

Tenderly he guided her up the stairs. The song changed. Their clue, Jim and Adelia started up the isle. She caught a glimpse of Max sitting next to Sally on folding chairs near the back of the church wishing Max were following her up the middle isle to the front pew on the grooms side. Her eyes moistened and she took a deep breath. Her tears were not for her son but for herself.

The wedding over Andrew stood between the mothers in the receiving line at the back of the church. Many limp handshakes, smiles, compliments about the music, the flowers, the beautiful bride, the handsome groom, the charming bride's maids, the ushers. The wedding had been a show. Six bride's maids in soft flowing gowns of pastel green; captivating music of a string quartet; the grand old church with its marble pillars and stained glass windows; Jane and Charlie a most handsome couple everything nearly perfect.

Adelia was surprised at the number of guests she recognized. Continually she learned of the thread with which Iowans were joined. She thought of Charlie's warning to be careful who she talked about until she learned the families because she might be insulting somebody's brother. He told her everyone in Iowa was related or related to someone who was related. She was finding him right.

CHAPTER XXIX

the groom, my son
always my child, my family
but today he gained other
family, her mother, her father
her aunt, her cousins,
her brothers and sisters
and I must share him
envious I know how thin
the rope now is I pray
it may strengthen
strand by strand
but they are not his biological family
and I will always be

ADELIA HOGAN

The three-story restaurant on Pocahontas Point was draped in green bunting. Three scrubbed college men in rented uniforms parked cars. Baskets of daisies decorated the lower floor where waiters in white tails passed campaign on Elizabeth's silver trays.

Elizabeth came to Adelia when she entered and squeezed her hand. "This reception will be talked about for years. Without your check it couldn't have been." Adelia smiled, felt smug. She sensed the awe of entering guests and gathered few parties of this magnitude had been hosted here.

Sherman Adams III, Charlie's room mate his freshman year at Virginia, the best man, toasted the couple and Jane's parents, and brother and sisters-in-law and sister and aunts and uncle and finally Adelia Charlie's only family.

Upstairs on the round tables covered with starched linens cloths place cards announced seating. Dinner started with pate, followed by consume, then salad before beef tenderloin and swordfish and white and red wine. The fourth course finished a stooped man dressed in all white cloths and a tall cook's hat wheeled in a ten-tier wedding cake. Jane and Charlie cut one piece. Cameras snapped and there were pictures and more pictures before the waitress cut and served cake to the three hundred guests.

Adelia had lost tract of the glasses of campaign and wine. She watched Jane and Charlie dancing their joy contagious yet she felt abandon. The older guests were leaving. The band started playing faster songs. She felt a hand on her shoulder and turned to a smiling Max.

"My dance, the mother of the groom must dance with me," he whispered leading her to the dance floor. Ellie winked at her from a near by table. She hoped no one else noticed how close Max held her all the time talking softly about his joy in having found her. When she thought she could no longer dance the strength in his arms as he led her across the floor convinced her otherwise.

Sally had left with Max's car. Adelia drank too much wine to be driving. Max turned the Bravada south not north when they left the reception. Adelia said nothing. Looking at the kind face of the man driving she thought of a different life, one that maybe could have been, if she had not retreated to her private place, been honest, not bashful and afraid to ask for help.

Max turned on the Dam road and when it dead-ended turned off the ignition.

"Why are you stopping here?" she queried.

"We did one hot night in our youth."

"Only to French kiss."

"You remember it all."

"Yes, but now we are adults."

"So."

"You say this is a small place. People wonder."

"I don't care."

"You care or we wouldn't be hidden on this dead end road."

"I'm here because you care."

She wanted to ask about the girl at the coffee shop before she felt his warm lips. The seats in the back were flat. He led her there. Only when the sun was a glow of pink in the eastern horizon did they dress. She dropped him off in the alley behind the Post Office in Okoboji. He knew day after tomorrow she was returning to Chicago but neither one had talked about it. Before he closed the door of the Bravada Max squeezed her hand and said, "if only you would stay."

She wanted to ask what he would do if she did. Would he divorce Sally and marry her or would they only meet on dead end roads and in secluded places? She didn't ask any questions instead she said in a quiet voice, "Good by."

"I love you." He was gone.

Driving home to sleep his last words echoed in her head. He could destroy her defenses. She loved him. She wished she could be certain he loved her not her money. Tears ran down her cheeks. She was a fool.

CHAPTER XXX

in a sea of bodies
a glut of talents
recognition rare
yet where the
population is sparse
recognition comes
does one try harder?
where there is love
not empty loneliness
in throngs of people

Adelia Hogan

Max never far from her thoughts Adelia sat on the dock finishing a mug of hot morning coffee and basking in the sun a gentle breeze off the water tickling her face. She spent most of her next to last morning in Iowa on the porch writing lines of poetry in her lined notebook wondering why she wanted to leave this place. She didn't hear Mr. Gilmore approach until he spoke. "People scheduled in the day after tomorrow canceled. Said to keep their deposit, just couldn't come. Cabin will be available until I drain the pipes in October. Hear anyone interested appreciate letting me know."

"Same rent?"

"About half, it is close to off season."

"I'll stay." Surprising herself Adelia went to get her checkbook. Returning with the check, she thought only of how to let Max know she was not leaving.

CHAPTER XXXI

Labor Day Swim
the hot days of the summer
when the temperatures reached three digits
and the old timers said
it had not been this hot since they drank lemonade
squeezed
from lemons and cooled with ice chipped from
blocks
delivered by the ice man
finally on labor day i went swimming
the lake warmer than my bath
i waded on slimy rocks and swam
and paddled on a cushion for my exercise
and relief for stiff joints
and i tried to position muscles often dormant
like a machine rusting in the junk yard
even out of the water i felt clean and relaxed

ADELIA HOGAN

Labor day weekend came and went. Charlie and Jane returned from their wedding trip to International Falls. Elizabeth and Andrew returned to teaching. The young faces in the restaurants and shops returned to college and high school. Lakeshore Drive was nearly deserted and each morning Adelia was awakened by the barge or dock builders pulling docks and boat hoists from the lake. Mr. Gilmore piled split aged oak logs near her back porch. She brought new ones in every day and at night had a fire in the field stone fireplace. Every afternoon at a quarter past two Adelia and Agnes started a game of cribbage. Always Adelia wanted to asked Agnes about Max wishing, Agnes would tell Max she had stayed.

It had been over six weeks since Charlie and Jane's wedding. Mr. Gilmore asked her nearly every day when she was leaving. He talked about the frost coming and the need to drain the water pipes and secure the cottage for winter. Charlie and Jane didn't say it but Adelia knew they were anxious for the Bravada. They kept talking about her coming back for Christmas. Adelia should leave. Yet she could not think her time with Max was over. Like a schoolgirl with a crush she dreamed of him every night and thought of him every day.

By the middle of October he still had not appeared. Adelia unable to admit he would not retreated to her private place and dreamed of what could have been.

At six a.m. on the morning of October sixteenth the phone rang and Adelia heard Max say, "If you had told me you were staying I would not have gone out of state trying to get my financial affairs in order. I'm coming over tonight."

Surprised and uncertain whether to believe the explanation for his absence she quickly promised to prepare supper. Later asking herself if he were coming to see her for a loan knowing if he were she would give it to him. Even if doing so would be against her better judgment.

At the grocery Adelia asked the woman in white behind the meat counter for beef tenderloin and had her cut twenty ounces. The woman expertly trimmed the meat wrapping it in white butcher paper. Adelia found Maytag Blue Cheese, walnuts, unsalted butter, red and yellow and green peppers, fresh parsley, large garlic buds, carrots, flawless zucchini and the most virgin olive oil, rusk, cream cheese, sour cream, raspberries blue berries and strawberries. At the liquor store she selected wine, Pinot Noir, and a bottle of brandy.

The oven had been pre heated to five hundred degrees ready for the beef tenderloin. The fragrance of garlic and parsley sautéed in olive oil hung in the air when Max slipped in the back door and engulfed her in his arms. "The food smells almost as good as you do."

"You're hungry?"

"My soul for you but my body needs substance."

She put the tenderloin in the oven, turned it down to 400 and stirred the peppers and squash she had put there earlier with the parsley and garlic. Crisp greens waited in the refrigerator and she tossed them with fresh oregano and basil and pressed garlic buds dissolved in olive oil and fine wine vinegar before adding walnuts and crumbles of the Maytag blue cheese. The dinner truly was a success. Max raved about Adelia's cooking as they sipped stout coffee and relished rich cheesecake topped with a colorful medley of blue berries, strawberries and raspberries.

"If I had known you could cook like this I really would never have let you go," he remarked.

The comment bothered her. She wanted to remind him the first time they talked he said Karla said she was a great cook. Did he only say he had thought about her all those years? Did he really remember? Had he not found financing in his time away and would he ask her for financial help?

He interrupted her thoughts rising and going outside. Finally he called her to come and look at the oranges and pinks in the sunset. The sun completed its descent before they went inside where she started to remove the dishes from the table. He stopped her took her hand and led her to the bedroom. They made love slowly deliberately.

Adelia never knew why then after all those years she released her secret. Max had been talking about his depression and suddenly he switched to Charlie and how Charlie reminded him of himself when he was young. And then he talked sadly about his life's regret of not having children.

"You may have a child," Adelia said.

"Yea Sally."

Adelia should have let it drop. She almost did. She listened to his breathing for a while before she said.

"No, not Sally."

"Rex III doesn't count. I love him like a child I'm sure. I have loved all my dogs. Cried for days after I had to put them to sleep. Always said there won't be another but there always is."

"You may have a son."

"I said dogs don't count though you love them and they love you." Max's expression was one of amusement.

"Max," Adelia spoke softly.

"I don't like to joke about this. I'm more sensitive on this point then you realize."

She should have said no more, but instead she blurted out, "Charlie maybe your son."

He looked at her, his eyes penetrating the silence. "Adelia you said Charlie may be my son." His voice was flat. His expression was one she had never seen.

"Charlie may be your son." Adelia said it the second time surprised to hear the words coming from her mouth.

"Does?"

Adelia didn't let him finish his question. "Charlie does not know."

"And your hus"

Again she interrupted before he could go on. "I never told him but he knew Charlie was not his son. I thought I alone carried the secret and the guilt. Before he died, he relieved me of the guilt."

"Why are you saying this?"

She detected suspicion in his voice. "Remember the last afternoon of that summer? We made love for the first and only time in your boat?"

"I have never forgotten."

"On the trip home I counted. Knew it was the wrong time. Knew I couldn't handle a pregnancy. You had betrayed me. My grandmother died. I had no one. I had nothing. I went to work for Joe as a maid. I purposely seduced him. We made love. Four weeks later I told him I was pregnant. He was a lonesome man more than twenty-five years my senior. He said my youth brought him back to life. Joe said he loved me and we married. He had no children and was over joyed when Charlie was born. Charlie looked like you from the beginning. No chin and his ears had those funny little lobes. I wanted Charlie to look like you. Yet I tried to pretend he was Joe's son. I learned to pretend I was in love with Joe."

Why did you say he maybe my son? How could he have not have been? Who else could his father be?

"I have never told anyone but the day before I left the day we made love I went with Dr. Kettleson when he took the boys to camp. On the way home he raped me. He took my virginity. I didn't have it to give to you. I feared that Dr. Kettleson was Charlie's father. I didn't want to think he was but didn't now how I could be sure.

"He looks like me. He is my son. He doesn't look like that bastard Kettleson you have to see that."

"For years I wanted to think he looked like you that he was your son but I would never be sure but then the night of Kettleson's party I looked at him hard. I saw nothing of Charlie in him and then I heard a laugh I thought was Charlie's but it was yours and for the first time I really thought I had been right from the beginning that he was your son."

Adelia had expected Max's sympathy. Yet Max spoke with an anger she had never seen in him. "He is my son. You always had to know that. Why didn't you tell me? Why did you let that bastard Kettleson rape you. Why did you, you let another man raise my son?"

"Joe treated Charlie as his own. No one could have loved Charlie more or have been better to him."

"He is my son. I would have loved him more."

The look on Max's face frightened Adelia. "You let another man raise my son?" His anger built.

What had she done? "But you were not there. I had to do the best I could."

"I wasn't there because you didn't let me be there. You knew I loved you. Why didn't you tell me? I would have taken care of you both."

"How, you were still in high school?"

"I would have, believe me I would have."

He said nothing more but rose and dressed and left slamming the door hard.

Adelia cried uncontrollably. She had given Max her secret. Made him angry. Max did not understand how she married an old man to save him and to provide security for their child. Max didn't know about all the tears on her pillow. Max could ruin her; ruin Charlie and Jane. She stopped surprised by her concern for Jane.

"Come back Max Luc," she silently cried, "oh please come back."

His tires sped on the gravel drive as his car headed for the road. Finally putting on her robe she went outside and watched the last bit of sun descend and a transparent round full moon slide above the eastern hill. Windless the darkening sky brought a slight chill. The night unseasonably warm Adelia sat outside until small nates drove her in. The windows open she sat in the twilight wanting to capture the beauty of the night seeking therapy for her troubled soul. She was jolted by the motor of a powerboat approaching her dock and watched a figure jump out of the shadows and expertly loop the bowline around a dock post. Only then did she realize it was Charlie and she was thankful Max was not still with her.

Adelia made Charlie a sandwich with the remainder of the beef tenderloin. Then lemonade for both of them squeezing fresh lemons and mixing the juice with chilled boiled sugar syrup and ice. Charlie looked at the two dinner plates in the sink without comment. He sat with his mother on the front porch and while he ate the sandwich and they sipped lemonade he told her how important it had been to him that she came, stayed. Jane's family would never be his. Then he squeezed her and said, "Mom I'm glad I got you. I miss dad. Seems like I got cheated there and you did too. For all he did for us we never had him in his young years. That must have been hard for you mom." Charlie kissed her on the cheek. Adelia still numb did not respond. She retreated to her private place unable to share her secrets with her son. Max was Charlie's father. Max knew it. Her secret no longer safe she tried to tell Charlie what she had told Max but the words would not come. Lightening flashed in the northwest sky. Charlie said he must leave before the storm. He called later from his home to tell her he had forgotten his cap just before the thunder boomed and an eerie wind blew in from the north and the heavens poured hail then rain and lightening flashes revealed savage black storm clouds and the lake turned angry and wild.

CHAPTER XXXII

life hangs on a string
one does know how fragile
the string is until it breaks
then one is not prepared

The helicopter came from the west to Dickinson County Memorial Hospital to pick up a patient waiting in the echoing hospital hall just inside from the landing pad where the bird would descent and wait just long enough for a stretcher and a body before lifting off again for the hospital in Sioux City. Adelia awakened by the flap of the helicopter flying back west finally fell asleep when the shrill noise of the telephone bell woke her. Ellie calling, her voice tired and strained told Adelia she had been a passenger in John Holland's boat heading out from Smith's Bay after a dinner anxious to make it across the lake before the impending storm. No one in the Holland boat had seen the sleek ski boat driven by Dr. Kettleson. The boats collided. A stunned Kettleson told the rescuers Sally Luc had been his passenger. Sally had not been found. Holland had been life flighted to Sioux City.

"Adelia," Ellie said softly, "I went to tell Max. He is in shock. He never loved Sally yet he was good to her. I reminded him of that. Before I left, he called Charlie said he needed to talk to him."

"Oh," Adelia hung up the phone. She said nothing more but went to the couch and pulling her knees to her chest she shook with fear and retreated to her private place.

The shore patrol found the ski boat about noon the next day. Sally's body was not in or near it. For five days they drug the lake. Boats pulling nets and moving slowly in Smith's Bay where Kettleson's boat was found. On the sixth day while a memorial service was conducted at a funeral home in Milford a twelve-year-old boy walking his dog on the beach near Pillsbury Point stumbled on Sally's remains.

All the time Adelia stayed sequestered in Tennessee. Charlie called on the second day saying Max called asking him to come and talk to him and he was going. Adelia spent the day in emotional turmoil and physical pain. Too numb to pen her poems she walked five miles and then took to bed covering herself with a big quilt though the day was hot.

Charlie called about ten. He had just left Max. He said Max had legal questions. Charlie said Max thanked him for his answers and told him he was a comfort. "It was strange, mother. I hardly knew him before I went. He talked to me as though we were dear friends. I left feeling a kinship with him."

She wanted to ask Charlie if Max had told Charlie he was his son? She wanted to know exactly what Max had said even though Charlie's voice did not reveal startling revelations.

The next morning Adelia went to the Flower Basket. Not recognizing the girl at the counter she ordered a large vase of daisies delivered to Max. She paid with cash and included an unsigned sympathy card.

Ellie called later to have Adelia join her at Broadway Brew for coffee. Adelia regretted claiming to have a headache. Ellie soon arrived at her door with three packages of tulip bulbs and a bag of bone meal. Adelia found a place near the south side of the garage where the soil was black and moist. With a pitchfork borrowed from Mr. Gilmore she dug in the dirt and loosened it before planting the bulbs in the trench she formed with her bare hands. The dirt between her fingers felt good. She covered the bulbs with half the bag of bone meal and then dirt before watering the area gently with the spray of the green garden hose. Standing over the plot holding the garden hose, she gazed at the sky a vivid baby blue ocean peppered with fluffy white snips of clouds a simple background for the oak, maple and box elder, and cottonwood leaves. Their green now touched with hues of red and gold and brown.

People planted bulbs in the fall to enjoy their flowers in the spring. People who were coming back planted bulbs. Adelia was not coming back. But the cottage needed flowers and they would be her gift. A thank you to the place where in three short months she had found brief happiness and defeating grief.

She returned the pitchfork and took the rest of the bone meal in the house. She washed her hands with squirts of liquid soap. Finally her finger nails washed clean of dirt she poured a glass of chilled White Burgundy. Taking it to the front porch she fixed her gaze on the mirror smooth lake and tried to rid her mind of all possible thoughts. She would go back to Chicago as soon as she could. She would send tickets for Charlie and Jane to visit her there. She did not belong here. Adelia could never return to Okoboji.

Two days later Adelia drove the Bravada with Jane ninety miles to the Sioux Falls, South Dakota Airport. She gave Jane the keys and a kiss and took a flight home.

She found Chicago bigger than she remembered and the traffic faster. Her body was in Illinois but her heart seemed elsewhere. Every day she wrote a post card to Agnes, each one with a different picture. She talked about the weather, politics, and the latest fashions. There were never words about herself or what she was doing. Never did she share her emptiness. One day she found in her mailbox a printed note thanking her for her sympathy. At the bottom the words in a scrawl "The daisies brought me comfort. Max". The note renewed her guilt. She wanted to respond but would not.

Charlie and Jane wrote infrequently but called often and she called them. From the day she got home they talked about her coming for Christmas. Charlie started asking specifically when she was coming in early November. Adelia said she was not coming. Jane came forth with the same questions near Thanksgiving. Adelia said she was not coming. They should come to Chicago.

Adelia spent Thanksgiving alone eating a frozen turkey dinner heated in the microwave. The Sunday after Ellie called. She would be at Okoboji with her family over the Christmas holidays and she was anxious to be with Adelia. Adelia said she was not coming. Ellie admitted Charlie had put her up to the call.

The first week in December a call came from Jane. Adelia sensed trouble from the tone of her voice. She feared something happened to Charlie but it was Jane's mother. Elizabeth diagnosed with lung cancer had less than three months to live. Jane said it would mean a lot to her mother to have her family and Adelia there for Christmas.

Adelia could not say no and the next day she purchased a flight to Minneapolis. Jane promised to pick her up there.

CHAPTER XXXIII

God we pray for
understanding not condemnation
forgiveness not revenge
love not hate.

Help us seek solutions
through study and debate
not by application of
our own preconceived
notions of righteousness.

Though we detest the act of violence
give us the wisdom to have compassion
for the actor and to look for reasons
for the behavior.

You have told us we are all
brothers and sisters and
families should love unconditionally.
Please show us how for only then
will we find true peace.

ADELIA HOGAN

Adelia's plane landed at the Minneapolis Saint Paul Airport at ten thirty on the morning of December twenty-third. Jane was waiting for her by the luggage carousal. The people of Minneapolis like those in Chicago dressed for cold weather, many wool hats, down filled coats, heavy mufflers and oversized boots. Outside there was a dusting of snow on the street and the weatherman on the Bravada radio promised more.

Adelia and Jane stopped at the Mall of American and with a mass of late shoppers did some last minute Christmas buying. They had a late lunch before Jane began the drive south and west to Okoboji. Adelia enjoying the day realized why mothers loved daughters.

Jane snapped the tape of a current novel in the cassette player. In Mankato Minnesota she turned it off and started talking. She told Adelia how she and Charlie were working with the young people at the church on a program aimed at convincing them they should avoid pre-martial sex. There was much Adelia wanted to tell Jane when she finished but she just said, "lets finish the tape."

The tape finished as they drove through the town of Spirit Lake. Jane started talking about how well Mr. Holland recovered from the boat accident. Adelia was hardly listening when Jane said, "There are rumors Max has been seeing Ellie."

Adelia could not have believed the jealous rage the words brought. Her worst fears were correct. Max had not wanted her. He had wanted her money. Ellie had money and now that he was free he could court Ellie in the open. They would make a respectable match. Not one behind closed doors or in the back of a car. Lake people need lake people Ellie would say. There was not another word said until they pulled in the driveway.

CHAPTER XXXIV

Adelia had not expected to see Max Lux sitting next to Charlie. Big yellow Rex III lounged at their feet. The coals in the fire place bright red lit their faces and high lighted their resemblance. Adelia managed a smile but inside the panic began to build.

Max said nothing but his slate blue eyes seemed to penetrate her being. Adelia sat and looked in the fire afraid to look in his eyes. Was Max out to claim both her son and her best friend?

Charlie served hot buttered rum in strong heavy mugs. As she sipped the sweet liquid Adelia relaxed a bit and she was starting to feel better when sweet voices outside singing *Silent Night* drifted inside and Jane went to the door. Fifteen or so youngsters about eight-grade age stood with smiles and rosy cheeks holding a big box for Jane and Charlie. Jane asked them in but cars waited and they said they had other places to go.

Inside the box was a basket of cheese and a card signed with twenty-one young signatures. Charlie explained to his mother and Max the sign-ers were members of their church class. He said he and Jane had talked to them last week about the need to avoid pre-martial sex. They told them about the physical and emotional risk they took if they engaged in it. He said the children talked openly. Jane smiled and spoke about explaining to the young people that she and Charlie had waited and not regretted it.

Max and Adelia listened their eyes down. Charlie served more hot buttered rum and popped popcorn over the fire. At ten Max talked about going home. Jane pulled out the sleeper in the office and insisted he stay the night. He readily consented recognizing he had consumed too much alcohol to be a safe driver.

Charlie had put Adelia's bags in what had become a bedroom behind the kitchen. She unpacked a few things but decided to wait until morning for a bath and quickly fell asleep. At four she was awakened to find Max sitting on the side of her bed his slate blue eyes smiling tenderly, "Adelia."

"Did you tell Charlie?" she immediately queried.

"No, I would not. His mothers honor is too important."

"Thank you, Max," she looked directly in his eyes. "I shall always be grateful to you for this. I shall never forget."

"I bribed Charlie to ask me here tonight. I was in his office when I heard his legal assistant say you were coming. I promised to buy an E Boat with him. I told him we would sail together. Race it. He is anxious."

Adelia surprised herself with a laugh. "Do I remember your using your sailing skills as a bribe before?"

"It was cheaper with Billie. His mother hadn't taught him to drive such a hard bargain." They sat quietly Adelia uncertain what he was saying. Was he trying to get close to Charlie and if he did and if the two men spent hours sailing on the lake someday after beers would Max reveal her secret? Or was Max here because she had come. If he was why was he seeing Ellie? Adelia wanted so badly for him to be here to see her she was afraid she was letting herself think false thoughts.

"Jane said there are rumors about you and Ellie." The words out she could not believe she said them.

"So be it Adelia—there are rumors, people here gossip—the fact they do may be the fear that keeps our area honest."

He had not said the rumors were not true. They must be true or he would have said they were not.

Max continued, "Mother told me yesterday a friend who lives in Chicago is coming at three o'clock this afternoon to play cribbage. Mother suggested I stop and meet her. Says she is a lovely widow about my age. Mother tells me I have been too lonesome since Sally's death. Hell I have been lonesome for thirty years."

"Your mother is a wonderful lady." Adelia tried to change the subject.

"No question about it and tomorrow in the lobby of the nursing home in front of the aids, guests and those residents who still have a bit of their senses she will introduce me to the lady who came from Chicago. The lady will say she is glad to be formally introduced and at the nurses station I will thank my mother's friend for her kindness to my mother and invite her to have dinner with me to say thank you."

"Is that honest?"

"No deceit, just things unsaid." The dog came in the room. Max scratched his ears. Rex and I are going home now the alcohol has made its way through my body."

"Why were you in Charlie's office?" There were things here she had to know.

"Charlie is my attorney. Kettleson and Holland's insurance companies offered substantial settlements for Sally's death. I didn't want money for her life. Charlie knew that but convinced me I should take it. I did it more for mother than for me. With Sally's help I had spent the money that was to pay for mother's care."

"You.."

He interrupted her. "I don't have to justify it to anybody. I was legally entitled to the money. But as unhappy as I was in my marriage to Sally, I didn't want her dead. When she was, I wasn't ready to take money for it. Charlie earned a substantial fee. I gave it to him on a fifty per cent contingency. It is twice as much as he even suggested, but I owed him that. I have never given him anything else."

She should say something, but she did not know what it could be. She wasn't certain how she felt about anything right now. Did he feel he had discharged any obligation he had to her or Charlie with the fee? Was he now truly free to form a relationship with Ellie?

"Charlie is my attorney now not the woman you saw me with last summer at the coffee shop. I was talking bankruptcy that day. She came from Sioux City."

"Your didn't need to explain." Adelia replied glad that he had explained.

Max spoke, "I did. I saw it bothered you. It bothered me but

"Enough Max. I don't need to know."

"You need to know everything. I don't believe in secrets. But tonight is not the time."

Ever so gently Max touched Adelia's cheek sending soft waves of passion through her body. She reached for him but he backed way.

"Don't or I can't leave. Our son wouldn't want his widowed mother sleeping with a widower in his house."

"Why could we not have had the will power Charlie and Jane did? Why then did we?"

He did not wait for her to finish. "I loved you then and I still do. Remember if we had not made love Charlie would not be. He and Jane are right. It was wrong for us. If we had waited we would be together now. You could have gone to college. You paid the price and I married the wrong woman."

"That night I told you about Charlie you were so angry."

"I was wrong. I didn't understand or appreciate what you did. I gained a son and lost a wife that night. I didn't love Sally." He looked in Adelia's eyes before he continued, "I didn't want her dead. There were good things about Sally"

"I understand." For the second time Max had expressed his remorse at Sally's death. Adelia did understand. She had gained deep affection for Joe but was never sure it was love. Yet looking at him in his casket she had deep remorse and she saw only the good things about their marriage not the bad.

Max continued, "I have never quit thinking of us."

Adelia heard the back door close and Max's car start. She lay listening to the December wind shake the trees for a long time after Max left the words "our son" echoing in her head.

She had slept little when she heard noise in the kitchen and with surprise noted it was eight o'clock. She promised Charlie she would make her traditional vegetable hash. He told her before she went to bed he purchased the ingredients and they waited in the vegetable bin of the refrigerator.

Adelia found the vegetables and a knife and she chopped and boiled potatoes, onion, carrots, turnips while she sautéed fresh parsley, oregano and basil in virgin olive oil before adding bits of red and green and yellow peppers and celery and frozen sweet corn. When the boiled mixture was soft, she drained it and added it and three kinds of cheese to the sautéed vegetables in the big cast iron skillet. The hash nearly cooked Jane came in the kitchen raving about the smell while she made a pot of strong coffee.

Charlie and Adelia and Jane ate all the hash and then lingered over coffee. It was a comfortable time until Jane mentioned her mother had a bad report from the doctor earlier in the week. Adelia saw her pain. She wished she could help ease it. "The good thing is she has quit smoking," Jane said. "It just came too late."

Adelia unpacked. Nothing she had brought seemed right so at a Spirit Lake woman's clothing store called the Cloths Peddler she selected a pink soft wool skirt and shell, a pink flowered scarf. At another shop Adelia brought dried fruit for Agnes who was waiting for Adelia in her room when Adelia reached the care center.

"You look radiant my dear."

"I'm going to take you to the lobby to see the tree."

Adelia stood behind Agnes' wheel chair. The two women were admiring the tree and the ornaments made by the sixth grade class at Okoboji School when a voice behind said, "Mother." The women turned. Agnes embraced her son.

"Max this is my friend Adelia Hogan. Adelia my son Max."

"Hello," Max and Adelia said in unison.

The Luther League from Saint Peter's Lutheran Church sang Christmas carols while the three played cribbage in the lobby. Max claimed to have played before but had forgotten the game. The women gently coached him until he beat them both. An aid came to remind Agnes dinner, was in five minutes. Adelia and Max started out together. "You have been so dear to my mother. I would like to invite you to dinner," he said in a loud voice as they passed the nurses station.

At a steak house that evening Adelia and Max shared a sirloin for two and a bottle of expensive wine and held hands with under the table. That night the temperature suddenly dropped nearly thirty degrees. The cold wind found every crack in Jane and Charlie's house. Adelia certain she had never been so cold retired early borrowing an extra quilt. She had drifted off when she heard a boom. The noise continued through the night. The next morning Charlie explained it was the sound of the ice covering the lake expanding as the temperature lowered.

There was a Christmas Eve party at the Carey's friends of Jane. Carey's three-story house on Fort Dodge Point was decorated throughout with a warming fire in each of the house's three fireplaces. The guests came in families. A little girl in a red velvet dress chased a little boy in a black tux with a red bow tie running and sliding on the slick hardware floor. Adelia's eyes kept scanning wishing without admitting to her self she wanted Max to be here. Many faces familiar she did not remember names and stayed close to Jane. In the dining room a long narrow table dressed in immaculate white starched linen was decorated with evergreens and a red runner. Platters of thinly cut beef tenderloin and multi grain buns were quickly consumed as was the tart fruit soup and champagne punch.

Suddenly the noise seemed too much and Adelia retreated to a corner near a small fireplace. Staring at the blaze she became aware someone was behind her. Turning she looked Dr. Kettleson in the face. He said hello and tried to smile but his eyes were empty and sad. He started a monologue and Adelia knew he had been drinking for a long time. She said nothing only listened as he spoke of his despair. How he wished he had been true to Betty. He ruined that with his affairs and now he had a young wife and babies. She had only married him for his money and position. She hated his other children and his grandchildren and estranged his relationship with them. Next he started talking about it was his fault Sally Luc was dead. He went with her because they both needed someone their own age to talk to and be with. "When you marry a young woman she doesn't share your history or memories or the problems of aging," he snorted then and she hoped he had finished but he continued. "Sally and I had been sneaking off for years. Her husband was so blind he never knew."

He stumbled off leaving Adelia to wonder about what he had said and why he had said it to her. His presence again affirmed her conviction that he bore no resemblance to Charlie. She wondered why had he talked about Sally being his age when she was at least ten years younger than he. She remembered the woman at the Kettleson party who talked ever so briefly about Dr. Kettleson's looking at her. Dr. Kettleson talked about his problems with a young wife. He was so egotistical he never thought the relationship was difficult for her. That was where Joe was different. Joe sensed it was difficult for Adelia to be married to a man twenty-five years her senior. He did everything he could to make it easier. The disappointment she felt with herself for becoming pregnant and not going to college kept her from appreciating the many good things life had brought her. Finally mellowed with the sweet glow of champagne Charlie and Jane and Adelia returned home. Adelia feeling alone and unwanted until there was a knock on the door and Max joined them. Adelia not knowing, he had not been invited.

Adelia retired to the kitchen and made without measuring her traditional Christmas chowder, rich milk, cream, Tabasco and Worcester sauce, potatoes, shrimp, lobster, white fish and butter. She served it with small crackers, hot sour dough bread and butter and a platter of fresh cut vegetables. The four ate on a small table near the fire before Max left to spend the rest of the evening with his mother. Charlie and Jane went to the Abbot's to help ready the house for tomorrow's celebration. Adelia in bed thought how it would be to have Max sleeping beside her.

CHAPTER XXXV

On the day in late December
we observe the birth of the child
gather in celebration with family
extend greetings missed in other months
For the young there is excitement
anticipation and the surprises
For the old there are memories
some laced with sadness, some joyful
disappointments erased by time
For all there is the promise of the day
another year, new hopes and dreams
The child's blessing.

ADELIA HOGAN

It warmed Christmas morning and about eight o'clock big wet snowflakes started to fall quickly covering the ground with a blanket of pure white. "My mother always says pure white snow at Christmas is the infant's soul clean, immaculate and free from sin," Jane commented.

At ten thirty Adelia, Charlie and Jane knocked at Ellie's door ready for her traditional Christmas morning Irish coffee. Ellie's house littered with paper, toys and children smelled of cinnamon and pine needles. A twelve-foot flocked pine stood tall and white on black slate in the family room. Max sat by his mother on chairs near the fireplace where a fire roared and an array of stockings had been emptied. Max took Adelia's coat and gave her arm a squeeze saying, "Mother has been waiting to see you."

Adelia went to Agnes and pulled a chair close. The two women sat side-by-side watching the activity. Ellie's son-in-law brought them glass mugs of strong coffee topped with Irish whiskey and thick whipped crème. Agnes raised her glass before she started to drink, "A toast Adelia to our continued friendship. I feared you would never come back."

Adelia smiled and slowly sipped the sweet mellow liquid quickly experiencing the tranquility that comes only when one drinks an Irish coffee. She had her first in an Irish Pub in Kilkeny on a cold wet day and thought then she was in heaven.

Only when Agnes had drained her cup did she turn to Adelia and pat her hand.

Adelia was thinking of asking for a second coffee when Charlie approached, "we are due at Jane's parents for dinner in fifteen minutes."

Max heard him and retrieved Adelia's coat from an upstairs bedroom. "You will stay through New Years," he said softly as he helped her with the coat.

Uncertain if it were a command or question she gave an affirmative response.

The tree in the Abbot living room was piled high with presents. Tables and chairs had been brought from everywhere. The aroma in the air increased when Jane and her sister pulled a perfectly browned turkey of at least thirty pounds from the kitchen oven. The girls busied themselves fixing dinner while Elizabeth her arms and legs like match sticks tried to smile from the over stuffed chair where she sat in the center of activities. Adelia went to her. The women embraced and tears formed in Adelia's eyes when Elizabeth whispered, "Jane still needs a mother. I rest easy knowing you will be there for her."

Adelia had a third though small helping of the turkey, mashed potatoes and dressing. There was mince, pumpkin, blueberry and Concord grape pie as well as cheesecake waiting for desert. Some opted for more wine or after dinner liquors and then the opening of presents began. Never had Adelia been a part of such Christmas festivity. The ohs and ah and love flowed. Presents selected carefully were appreciated though few were expensive. Uncertain what to purchase Adelia gave crisp new bills. She felt sheepish when she realized the care with which her presents had been picked. Yet the smiles and warm words of thanks convinced her the money was both needed and appreciated. The Abbotts made her feel good about her generosity.

Elizabeth and Andrew gave Adelia a collage of wedding snapshots with flattering pictures of her. There was a book of poetry by Walt Whitman, another by Ogden Nash and a blank bound book for writing her poetry from the rest of the family. Charlie chose a handsome piece of luggage for his mother. Jane gave Adelia a copy of the story she wrote about meeting Charlie and her special memories of Joe and Adelia. Adelia found herself fighting back tears. The love contagious she felt only she was truly alone.

Max called and talked to Andrew before asking for Adelia. "New Years," We will watch the Victory Bowl with Andrew and Elizabeth. The University of Iowa Hawkeyes are playing. Everybody in Iowa watches the Hawks."

CHAPTER XXXVI

They say kissing one on new years eve is a sign of happiness for the year, that is if you kiss the right one

After the game Max and Adelia left Elizabeth and Andrew and went to the restaurant on Pocahontas Point where the wedding reception had been held. They had asked the Abbots to join them. Elizabeth was too weak. A nurse was there with her but Andrew said he could not leave her fearful when he returned she would be gone. The dedication the Abbots had to each other had always been evident to Adelia. And now she saw them hanging onto each last moment. They had years of true love and the rewards that came with it. Where there was that much love the one left to mourn had to be devastated.

Max and Adelia said little on the drive to the restaurant. Adelia sensed Max too was groping with grief. Finally he spoke, "It will be harder for Andrew to lose his spouse than it was for us?"

"Max, he won't have regrets. We both did. But he loves her so. Only when I am with you do I understand what love really is. There would be no reason for me to live if you were dead."

She took his hand, squeeze it and kissed him on the cheek. Words were not an adequate response. He had never been out of her thoughts since they first sat on the state pier eating cherries. Until today she had not admitted it to herself but the dream of meeting him again had sustained her in her marriage to a man too old to be her husband. She would not want to live if Max were dead."

"Be careful," I'll drive in the ditch," Max shouted as she kissed his cheek. They both laughed. Their laughter a brief release from the sorrow they felt for Andrew and Elizabeth.

Adelia and Max ate rare prime rib and lobster and sat at a small table for two and stared in each other's eyes. The car radio was on and midnight approached as Max drove Adelia back to Charlie's. He stopped behind the garage as the announcer announced the entry of the New Year and the familiar music of *Auld Lang Syne* blared from the speaker.

"This acquaintance will never be forgot," Max, said pulling her close. Adelia shivered. He kissed her passionately and in his arms and feeling his lips on hers the years between then and now melted. For a moment she thought herself still a young girl with dreams of an exciting love. He held her tighter and kissed her again. "I said we would be married, remember?"

She nodded.

"I decided you would be my wife the day I saw you picking Bing cherries from the wooden crate at the Arnolds Park Grocery. I didn't think it would take over three decades to marry you."

Adelia smiled as Max continued, "All I want to know is how soon can it happen? I'm thinking only weeks, maybe days or minutes."

Adelia kissed his forehead, scratched behind his ears, "months Max but not years."

Elizabeth died on January third. Her funeral was at St. Joseph's three days later. There was standing room only in the big church filled with friends, former students and family. She was buried in a pretty cemetery overlooking East Okoboji. Afterward the Ladies of St. Joseph's served a ham and potato casserole, Jell-O salad cake and coffee in the big church basement.

Adelia who tried to be strong for Jane saw a joy amidst the sorrow. The Mass and the dinner were a celebration of Elizabeth's life. People in this part of Iowa went to funerals. They were not too busy. In seeing death they seemed to prepare themselves for when it came to them. Unlike the city where one ignored it until it hit you and then others ignored you. This place where people knew each other's names and cared and gossiped about one another was where Adelia wanted to be. She would always be looked at as coming from Chicago. Her ancestors were not Iowa pioneers. Her son's were though he did not know it. The spirits of the lake brought them both here. The hand of friendship was quickly extended. She was almost part of the family and it gave her great comfort.

She looked at Jane at her father's side listening to yet another former student of Elizabeth say a nice thing about her and she knew she loved Jane, the girl she had once hated. Someone said love and hate are closely related. That had to be. Adelia never felt for any person the hate she once felt for Jane. How that all had changed. Jane turned to Adelia then and the two women embraced and sobbed in each other's arms.

When they regained their composure, they turned to see Ellie and Andrew sharing a story about Elizabeth and for the first time since Adelia returned she saw Andrew smile.

Adelia returned home four days later and began the difficult task of preparing to move. Every day she made difficult decisions. Every night she waited for Max's nightly phone calls. If he had not called by nine, she called him. On the few nights he did not answer she found herself worrying about him.

In February Adelia again made arrangements to rent Tennessee. In early April she arrived in Okoboji. She wore long underwear and wool slack and sweaters and heavy wool socks and she kept the fireplace burning constantly to keep warm. She saw the first stems of the tulips she planted by the garage emerge even before all the small piles of hard snow had melted. She watched the ice on the lake blacken and sink.

As April turned to May she sensed excitement and anticipation penetrated the area. Dock builders waited for nearly windless days to begin their labor and quickly long wooden piers extended from every lot into cool clear water. Barges with cranes came then and with the precision of craftsmen the cranes gently lifted boat hoists that had wintered on the lakeshore. The cranes swung the hoists high over the shore placing them delicately next to the docks.

Adelia felt the celebration, anticipation and welcoming of spring. Little buildings along the highway were gaining new life. Signs announced new businesses and paintbrushes were seen everywhere.

On Broadway Street Adelia stopped at Broadway Brew looking for coffee and found the shop being enlarged and remodeled. Katie directing the crew promised her coffee and a hot cinnamon roll the Saturday morning of Memorial Day Week-end. Then she invited Adelia in to share for a moment the banter of the young bodies who all seemed to have grown up at Okoboji and were seeking as Ellie said to reclaim its magic.

One morning at the Okoboji Post Office where the population increased each morning and the new faces spoke of Arizona, California and Florida winters Adelia asked the man in blue work cloths with the logo of a local marina whose mail box was next to hers why the piers and boat lifts were not just left in the water all winter long.

His usual smile changed to one of authority and wisdom. He looked at her in the way people look at the unknowing and said very slowly least she not understand, "lady, the lake freezes. They would be frozen in. Then when the ice broke up in the spring and the ice floats were blown by the wind they would tear up any dock or boat hoist left to winter in the lake.

Adelia said nothing more.

Max's real estate sales booming they spent as much time together as they could. Charlie and Jane arrived one night while she sat before the fire writing poetry. Smug smiles on their faces they told her in late November she would be a grandmother. Adelia started looking at baby cloths and furniture and buying more cloths than any six newborn babies could ever use. She kept the clothing in a top dresser drawer and took it out frequently to look at and dream of rocking her new grandchild.

On Mother's day Max and Adelia took Jane and Charlie and Agnes to a restaurant on the West side of West Okoboji for Sunday brunch. Max ordered champagne. After it was poured for everyone but Jane who refused because of her pregnancy Max toasted his mother and his wife to be and her family. He smiled in a strange way and added, "her family will become mine after our wedding at summer's end."

The next week Ellie took Adelia to Minneapolis where she found a floor length ivory lace gown and a matching lace mantilla.

One Tuesday evening while Max showed an expensive West Okoboji house Ellie and Adelia sat on the porch at Broadway Brew discussing the wedding and watching teenagers gather for a teen dance at Murphy's.

Adelia and Ellie had finished their coffee and were ready to leave when Ellie said, "Adelia I have something to tell you. I know it is premature but Andrew and I have been spending sometime together."

"Oh."

"Jane and Charlie don't know. He is worried about what his children will think."

"He has to be very lonesome."

"He is. We both loved Elizabeth. We share that and other things."

"And."

"I look at you. After Sally was killed Max and I spent time together. He was always talking about you. He wanted to pursue you but was afraid it wouldn't look right. I told him we were getting older and he shouldn't wait. He loves you so much. I don't know when he started loving you, but I think it happened long before I knew you. Maybe someday you'll share the secret."

"Ellie you think"

"Adelia I think that Andrew and I are in love. He has loved. I have not. But he can show me how."

Adelia smiled. "I'll work on making Jane and Charlie understand." Ellie had said nothing about Andrew wanting her money. Adelia felt smug. Ellie was learning as she had that even at their age a woman could be loved for who she was and not for her money.

A boy and girl walked by arm and arm on their way to Murphy's. "I'm glad Murphy has dances for our young people," Ellie commented. "The population in Okoboji is graying. Our generation returns because of sweet memories of youth. If those kids at the dances have their memories, they too will come back with their children."

CHAPTER XXXVII

We each are afforded a bit of beauty, a bit of love,
a bit of happiness.
And we are given a bit of worry, a bit of sorrow,
and a bit of grief.
It is our responsibility to balance them all
and be neither over whelmed nor
under whelmed
to cherish the good
accept the bad
love and forgive our fellow man.

ADELIA HOGAN

An umbrella decorated the table in the dining room at Lakeview and a ribbon strung above the table said "Best Wishes Adelia." Everyone in the room knew the story of how Agnes introduced her friend Adelia to her son and how they would marry in August. Yet Agnes insisted on telling it again and again. She finished smiling the smug smile of a mother, who had just found a prize for her son. Adelia tried to silence her, more embarrassed each time it was told. There being no retreat she finally accepted her plight and patted Agnes's hand.

"I should have brought my camera," Jane commented looking at the gathered residents who today all wore bright colored clothing and smiled.

An aid just coming in heard her and returned with the cardboard kind of camera with the flash. "We keep 'em. Nobody thinks of bringing a camera to an old folks home. They git here and decide it might be the last time to take pictures."

Jane cringed at the girl's honesty. Agnes had been at Lakeview long enough to take the girls comment in stride.

CHAPTER XXXVIII

> *rarely in a lifetime do dreams really come true*
> *sometimes when they do, they are not happy*
> *but the time they come true and are happy*
> *is life's greatest gift.*

ADELIA HOGAN

Adelia walked through Tennessee saying good-by. Two suit cases and one battered blue Samsonite train case waited on the porch Charlie having promised to deliver them to the house Max had chosen for he and Adelia on Des Moines Beach. Adelia had wanted a home on Haywards Bay, but so did everybody else and there was nothing for sale. She hoped perhaps someday soon Mr. Gilmore would sell the cottage and they could build a new house there among the oaks with big porches to enjoy the lake view.

The sky was lightening though Adelia did not see the sun. The garden store delivered a trellis adorned with pastel daisies and placed it on a green knoll over looking the lake. Norman Montgomery, a district court judge and Max's boyhood friend who agreed to perform the ceremony was ten minutes late. The three stood backs to the arch on the bank. The starting gun sounded during the ceremony as sail boats racing in the Sunday series of the Okoboji Yacht Club races crossed the imaginary line.

Adelia and Max recited vows they had written both stumbling and wishing they had not attempted to memorize the words. A thin blond girl in a loosely woven beige dress and a young man who had to have been her brother sang an Irish love song to the sweet music of their guitars. Adelia hardly heard the words. Finally Norman declared with the authority granted him by the state of Iowa he pronounced them man and wife. Max gently kissed her. The guests clapped. Charlie and Jane wiped tears from their eyes and a noisy boat pulling a water skier entered the bay.

Max and Adelia stood arm in arm the gentle lake breeze blowing their hair accepting congratulations and best wishes and comments how much Charlie looked like he could be Max's son.

Afterwards the invited guests went with the couple to their new home on Des Moines Beach. The guests toasted them with champagne. Max and Adelia stood and toasted each other from a single long stemmed glass etched with the word *Mission.* Everyone ate little mushroom caps filled with spicy sausage and tiny crème puffs filled with crab salad before embarking on the table in the dinning room sporting baked egg dishes in silver bowls yellow and red peppers fried in spicy oil, small rounds of French toast with hot pure maple syrup, tiny sticky pecan rolls, country ham, wild rice and platters and bowels of fresh fruits and vegetables. The Beach Boys' music played softly in the background.

Adelia smiled seeing Andrew and Ellie sitting together at a small table sharing an intimate conversation. Finally Adelia and Max cut the three-tier wedding cake decorated with colorful daisies and thanked the guests as they filtered away.

After the full house emptied Max went to the refrigerator and removed a brown paper sack. Taking Adelia by the hand they walked with Rex III along the lakeshore to Arnolds Park, down Broadway Street, past Murphy's. At the pier they took off their shoes and sat dangling their feet in and the water. One by one they took the firm dark red cherries from the sack twisting off the stem and putting them in their mouth. After savoring the sweet firm meat they spit the seeds in the lake in a contest to see whose seed went further. They laughed, a laugh that tickled the belly, and warmed the soul. Adelia said a silent prayer in Thanksgiving for this chance for happiness and excitement.

The cherries eaten Max looked in the clear water. "Will the cherry tree never grow?" Adelia smiled and kissed his cheek before Rex moved between them.

They walked back to Murphy's. Rex found a place to lie outside by the door. Adelia and Max went in and sat on the stools at the long bar. A soft song played. They rose and danced on the wooden floor their bodies close. Neither saw Jane and Charlie enter, watch and leave hand and hand. Max and Adelia eyes closed only saw the Arnolds Park grocery store those many years ago. In that moment the magic of their youth was rediscovered.

The morning after the wedding Adelia and Max and Jane and Charlie attended seven o'clock weekday Mass at St. Joseph's.

After Mass the church emptied. Father O'Donnell called Adelia and Max to the altar. In the presence of Charlie and Jane Father blessed Adelia and Max's marriage thereby recognizing their union in the eyes of the Catholic Church.

That night for the first time Max and Adelia shared a martial bed. Their lovemaking was long. Not since the night of the boat accident had their bodies joined. Afterwards laying close in the dark night both knew this love belonged in marriage. Charlie and Jane had been right.

The last entry in Adelia's diary was written the next morning before she left their West Okoboji home. She wrote:

"Today I know true happiness. Last night my first and only true love and I consummated our marriage. We had first loved on the waters of West Okoboji and the promise of the water spirits brought me back to this place. My son too found the magic of the water spirits and came here to marry a wonderful girl. Now they are going to have a baby and Max and I are the child's biological grand parents so our family will live on. Some may say it is not magic but I believe it all is. I can ask no more from life than this and should my life be short I know that some day my soul and the soul of Max shall unit on the lake that brought me my true love.

IN THE BACK OF KAREN GOOD'S BOOK WAS WRITTEN

Charlie never said a word about the story. Everyday for a long time I wanted to ask him. I started writing a novel and poetry and they consumed my non-working hours. I realized too that in our many years of teaching my husband and I had grown apart. Or maybe we had never had a close relationship. I loved him. I always knew that but sometimes it seemed we were only two beings who lived in the same home. Then day-by-day Roger seemed more attentive to my needs. Maybe it was because I became more attentive to his. And there were tender times. Unlike any we had since our honeymoon.

We both missed the public school environment and some days found ourselves wishing to be back. But Roger found a good faculty at the community college and I continually found the work at Charlie's office more rewarding and at his suggestion I began a legal assistant's course. Charlie continued to give me more responsibility.

One day I was at Lakeview helping a resident sign what in legal terms was called a durable power of attorney meaning it was still good if the person signing it became mentally incompetent. The staff at Lakeview seemed happier and better dressed than I had ever seen them.

I walked by Agnes's room and remembered it had been a long time since Charlie sent me over to help Agnes. I wondered if he were no longer doing her work. Agnes looked up as I walked by. I hesitated to say anything least the work I had done with her had not been unsatisfactory and that was why Charlie did not send me to see her anymore. The smile Agnes gave convinced me that was not true. I returned the smile and paused for a moment in her door way. She bade me to enter.

I first caught sight of a new flowered bed spread and then noticed the walls of her room that once had been bare now were covered with the wedding pictures of Adelia and Max, Charlie and Jane and a series of pictures of their young daughter Adelia Elizabeth. She saw me looking at them and smiled. Only then did I see the manuscript I had given Charlie sitting on her bedside table. She put her hand on it gently turned her slate blue eyes towards me and said, "my family, our secret."

I nodded not certain how to reply and was grateful she started to talk. "I had given up. Max was killed. My life seemed over. I mourned for years that he had no descents. You get old. You want to know there will be part of you left. Then he was killed and I was consumed with the guilt of wishing for more.

One night about eight o'clock just as the shift was changing Charlie came alone to my room. Charlie had been good to me after Max died.

But it was like it was a duty. Remember he always sent you when I needed something. There were tears in Charlie's eyes and he called me grandmother and said he loved me. It was strange. I mean I thought it was because Max had been his stepfather. Then he handed me this manuscript and asked me to read it. My eyes are not good but I didn't sleep that night nor the next day until I had finished it. Maybe the story did not surprise me because I finished it knowing it was true.

Adelia Elizabeth has a grandmother now and I have a real family. Only Charlie and I know Adelia and Max's secret. We share the love of a family but have agreed to keep the secret ours. We have kept it too from Jane and our granddaughter Elizabeth Adelia; I trust you are the only stranger who knows our secret.

"I am," I responded not certain what I would have said if I had breached the confidence.

"My father would not have been surprise, about the force that brought Charlie here that is."

"Oh." It seemed so strange but I knew exactly what she meant.

"Nor am I my dear. There is magic here for all of us. Sometimes we don't look hard enough."

She pointed to a frame with three pictures of Charlie on her bedside table. I picked it up and only then did I realize only one picture was of Charlie. The other two were of men about thirty taken at different times.

"Charlie, Max and my brother," Agnes said.

I looked again at the pictures and any doubts about the truth of Adelia's story were erased.

As I started to leave Agnes stopped me. "There is a last thing you should know. Adelia left Charlie a fortune."

"I surmised that," I quickly replied.

"Did you notice how much happier the staff here is?"

"Yes," I assured her uncertain why she had brought it up.

"Well after reading what you have written Charlie established a trust with part of the income from the artificial hip his step father patented. The trust provides money for education opportunity, vacations and assistance for the medical workers in this county."

My smile was big while my eyes filled with tears.

Agnes smiled too. "Promise you'll come back for a game of cribbage."

"I don't play."

"I'll teach you."

"How about next Wednesday?"

"I'll be waiting," Agnes said before bidding me good-by.

Roger and I took a walk that night. We passed where the Peacock Lounge once stood on past where the merry-go-round and the little train once ran. The Roof Garden and the Fun House were gone. In its place was a museum filled with pictures of long ago; old boats and happy faces of once youthful lake residents now long dead. We walked to the State Pier higher and stronger than it was the night Roger and I met. We sat trying to dangle our feet to the water and looking out at the waves. I thought about all the generations who had loved the lake and the happiness and sadness the waves had washed away while the lake remained clear and blue, its personality changing with the weather. A boat cruised slowly by two young bodies close in the front seat. Behind it was a fishing boat with two older men and fishing gear.

The sun slipped beneath the horizon and as the lights came on the lake like a mirror reflected their beauty.

Roger gently took my hand pulled me close and kissed me then and there.

"There is a magic spirit in this lake darling," he said. "I look at you and see the twenty-one year old who left the Roof Garden because no one asked her to dance. I fell in love with you the minute I saw you. I was too bashful to talk. My life would never have been this full if you had not started the conversation. During the years between then and now I have forgotten to remind you how much I love you and how important you are to me. This lake constantly reminds me."

"I held Roger close looking in the clear water thinking maybe I would see a cherry tree taking root and finding in this short minute the magic of my thirteenth summer. The gentle lap of a boat wake caressed the shore. Roger pulled me closer to him. Hearing in my head the soft voice of the Indian Maiden singing a love song to the boy she once left behind I thought of the picture on Charlie's desk of Adelia and Max on their wedding day knowing they were hearing the love song too.

ELIZABETH ADELIA HOGAN'S STORY

Our sophomore history teacher Mr. Howell had us writing our family histories and I seemed to have problems putting my family history together. My mother had her genealogy tracing her family to before the Revolution. A grandfather with many greats fought in that war and she was a DAR on her father's side meaning a Daughter of the American Revolution. But I had little history of my father's family. His mother had been killed in an airplane crash before I was born and his father who was some twenty-five years older than his mother died in Chicago before my parents were married. I kept asking my father questions about his family and finally on my half birthday, when I was fifteen and one half, my father gave me a manuscript he said was written by his then legal secretary Karen Good nearly two decades earlier. He said what he was giving me was Karen's copy that she had given him several years earlier.

I knew Mrs. Good. Unlike some of the other people my father employed she always greeted me with a smile any day I came to his law office and made me feel special. I knew she was a grandmother and I always had wished she were mine because I didn't have just a plain grandmother. I had a step grandmother Ellie who married my mother's father after my mother's mother died. Ellie was nice to me and talked about how my father's mother had been a good friend but she had a number of grandchildren of her own who I knew came first as they should. And there was Agnes who my father once said was my great grandmother but when I asked him to explain the

157

connection he grew silent and said never mind. Agnes died when I was five and while she always treated me as a special person I never figured out how or if we were related.

The book answered many of my questions about my father's family and revealed to me family secrets long kept. It gave me an insight to times past when secrets were kept and young women were hesitant to report incidents of sexual abuse. It made me realize that premarital sex could result in grief and it made me proud to know my parents had avoided it.

It also cheered me to know there were others like I who believed there is a special magic in Lake West Okoboji. My parents' home has been on its shores for as long as I can remember. The lake with it multiple personalities has always been a part of my life. It is where I learned to swim, caught my first fish, won a number of sail boat races, and ice skated and ice boated on cold winter days. To me an only child it was a companion, a listener and a friend. I loved it multiple personalities and one of my greatest joy was to sit on my family's dock on a hot windless summer day and stare at the still blue water. No matter where my adult life may take me I know I will return to Okoboji often.

After reading the manuscript I asked my father's permission to show the manuscript to my teacher Mr. Howell. My father thought about my request for a spell before he gave me the permission I requested but conditioned it on my promise to make it clear to my teacher the manuscript was for his eyes alone and he did not have permission to show it to others.

Mr. Howell kept the manuscript for several months and when I asked about its return he gave it back to me and he told me it was a story that needed to be shared.

When I told my father what Mr. Howell had said he put on his stubborn face and said, "no way."

I found myself disagreeing with my father and told him so. Neither of us knew my mother who was always a peacemaker had entered the room and was witness to our conversation.

When she asked what was wrong I tried to get her to take my side but quickly realized she had never seen the manuscript either and asked my father if she could read it. He initially said no but she had her own way of changing his mind and finally he relented but in doing so told her she had to read the entire document and not be offended that my mother did not like her when they first met.

My mother took the manuscript and she must have read all night because at breakfast the next morning she was adamant the manuscript be printed as a book. My father finally agreed. The some names and places were changed but this book is the one Mrs. Good wrote.

Elizabeth Adelia Hogan

Made in the USA
Charleston, SC
03 May 2013